Praise for Award-Winning, National Bestselling Author JOAN HOHL

✳✳✳   ✳✳✳

"A compelling storyteller who weaves her tales with verve, passion and style."
> —*New York Times* bestselling author
> Nora Roberts

"Joan Hohl is a top gun!"
> —*New York Times* bestselling author
> Catherine Coulter

"Writers come and writers go. Few have the staying power, the enthusiastic following, of Joan Hohl. That's talent!"
> —*New York Times* bestselling author
> Kasey Michaels

✳✳✳   ✳✳✳

Don't miss Mitch's story—he's the brother of Adam Grainger, the hero from Joan Hohl's *A Memorable Man* (Silhouette Desire #1075)

Dear Reader,

Thanks to all who have shared, in letters and at our Web site, eHarlequin.com, how much you love Silhouette Desire! One Web visitor told us, "When I was nineteen, this man broke my heart. So I picked up a Silhouette Desire and…lost myself in other people's happiness, sorrow, desire.… Guys came and went and the books kept entertaining me." It is so gratifying to know how our books have touched and even changed your lives—especially with Silhouette celebrating our 20th anniversary in 2000.

The incomparable Joan Hohl dreamed up October's MAN OF THE MONTH. *The Dakota Man* is used to getting his way until he meets his match in a feisty jilted bride. And Anne Marie Winston offers you a *Rancher's Proposition*, which is part of the highly sensual Desire promotion BODY & SOUL.

First Comes Love is another sexy love story by Elizabeth Bevarly. A virgin finds an unexpected champion when she is rumored to be pregnant. The latest installment of the sensational Desire miniseries FORTUNE'S CHILDREN: THE GROOMS is *Fortune's Secret Child* by Shawna Delacorte. Maureen Child's popular BACHELOR BATTALION continues with *Marooned with a Marine*. And Joan Elliott Pickart returns to Desire with *Baby: MacAllister-Made*, part of her wonderful miniseries THE BABY BET.

So take your own emotional journey through our six new powerful, passionate, provocative love stories from Silhouette Desire—and keep sending us those letters and e-mails, sharing your enthusiasm for our books!

Enjoy!

Joan Marlow Golan

Joan Marlow Golan
Senior Editor, Silhouette Desire

Please address questions and book requests to:
Silhouette Reader Service
U.S.: 3010 Walden Ave., P.O. Box 1325, Buffalo, NY 14269
Canadian: P.O. Box 609, Fort Erie, Ont. L2A 5X3

The Dakota Man

JOAN HOHL

Published by Silhouette Books
America's Publisher of Contemporary Romance

To my dear Melissa,
the editor from…
heaven.

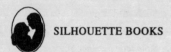

SILHOUETTE BOOKS

ISBN 0-373-76321-2

THE DAKOTA MAN

Visit Silhouette at www.eHarlequin.com

Printed in U.S.A.

Books by Joan Hohl

JOAN HOHL

is the bestselling author of almost three dozen books. She has received numerous awards for her work, including the Romance Writers of America's Golden Medallion award. In addition to contemporary romance, this prolific author also writes historical and time-travel romances. Joan lives in eastern Pennsylvania with her husband and family.

Dear Reader,

Twenty years!

Can you believe it? It seems impossible that twenty years have passed since Silhouette burst onto the publishing scene, astounding the industry with its immediate success, thrilling readers, like you and me, with fresh, absorbing and exciting love stories from the different lines—Special Edition, Desire, Intimate Moments—that evolved from the original Silhouette Romance.

And over these past twenty years, Silhouette has given its thousands—no, millions—of readers such gifted writers to craft those wonderful stories: Nora Roberts, Linda Howard, Diana Palmer, Elizabeth Lowell, Annette Broadrick, Kasey Michaels, Heather Graham Pozzessere and so many, many more.

I am both proud and honored to be counted among the numbers of Silhouette writers. And I sincerely hope you enjoy my offering to the celebratory year, *The Dakota Man.*

Twenty years! I still can't believe it.

It has been a spectacular twenty years.

Thanks for the great books, Silhouette.

And thank you, loyal readers, for making it all possible. We owe it all to you.

All my best,

One

His brow furrowed in a frown, his square jaw clenched and his lips sealed in an anger-tight thin line, Mitch Grainger sat at his desk and stared at the object cradled in the palm of his broad hand. He could only scowl at the brilliant, multi-faceted engagement ring of clustered pink diamonds, encircled by smaller rubies.

Less than an hour ago, Mitch had retrieved the ring from the floor near his desk. Which is where the object had landed after bouncing off his chest, hurled at him in unreasonable fury by Natalie Crane, the beautiful, cool, usually unemotional woman who had been his fiancée mere moments before.

The flawless gemstones caught the afternoon sun rays slanting through the window blinds behind him. Mitch made a soft sound that was part rude snort, part unpleasant laugh.

Women. Would he ever understand them? Had any man ever understood them? More to the point, Mitch mused, closing his fingers around the bauble, did he give a damn anymore?

Not for Natalie Crane, certainly, he thought, answering his own question. Without allowing him the courtesy of offering an explanation for the scene she'd witnessed, she had jumped to the wrong conclusion. Coldly calling him a cheat and telling him their engagement was over, she had thrown the ring at him.

Fortunately, Mitch had never deluded himself into believing he was in love with her; he wasn't and never had been. He had simply decided that, at the age of thirty-five, it was time to choose a wife. Natalie had appeared eminently suitable for the position, being from one of the most wealthy and prestigious families in the Deadwood, South Dakota, area.

But now Natalie was history. With her precipitous accusations, she had impugned his honor, and he forgave no one for that.

Honor, his personal honor, was the one standard Mitch held as absolute. He had believed Natalie knew the depths of his sense of honor. Apparently, he had been mistaken, or she never would have misconstrued the situation she had happened upon, immediately leaping to the erroneous conclusion that he was playing around behind her back with his secretary, Karla Singleton.

Poor Karla, Mitch thought, recalling the stricken look on his secretary's face after the scene. Shaking his head, he slid open the top desk drawer, carelessly tossed the ring inside and slammed it shut again. He had never really liked the token, anyway. The concoction of pink diamonds encircled by clustered rubies had been Natalie's choice; his preference had been a simple, if large, elegant two-and-a-half-carat, marquis-cut solitaire.

Poor, foolish Karla, he amended, heaving a sigh raised by both sympathy and impatience.

Mitch could understand passion, he had experienced it himself...quite often, truth to tell. But what he couldn't understand, would never understand, was why in hell any woman—or man, either, for that matter—would indulge their passions to the point that they'd risk their health as well as pregnancy through unprotected sex.

But believing herself in love, and loved in return, Karla had risked all with a man who had taken his pleasure…then taken off. He had supposedly left to find a job with a future, but nonetheless leaving Karla devastated, pregnant, unwed and ashamed to tell her parents.

Not knowing what else to do, Karla had turned to her employer, sobbing out her miserable tale of woe on Mitch's broad shoulder. Of course, Natalie had picked that moment to pay a visit to his office. She had witnessed him holding the weeping young woman in his comforting arms and heard just enough to erroneously conclude that, not only had he been fooling around with Karla, but that he had impregnated her, as well.

As if he would ever be that stupid.

In retrospect, Mitch figured it was all for the best, since he certainly didn't relish the thought of being married to a woman who didn't trust him implicitly. From all historical indications, marriage could work without depthless love, but in his considered opinion, it couldn't survive without trust.

So had ended his brainstorm of acquiring a wife, setting up house and having a family.

On reflection, Mitch acknowledged the niggling doubts he had been having lately about his choice of Natalie, not as a wife—he felt positive she would make an exemplary wife—but as the mother of his children. And Mitch did want children of his own some day. While he had admired Natalie's cool composure at first, he had recently begun to wonder if her air of detachment would extend to her children…his children.

Having grown up with two brothers and a sister, in a home that more often than not rang with the sound of boisterous kids, controlled by a mother who had always been loving, even when firm, Mitch desired a similar upbringing for his own progeny.

In all honesty, Mitch admitted to himself that he was more relieved than disappointed by the results of Natalie's false assumptions.

But he still had Karla's problem to contend with, for she had asked for his advice and help. Mitch had always been a sucker for a woman's tears, especially a woman he cared about. His own sister could give testimony to that. The sight of a woman he cared for in tears turned him, this supposedly tough, no-nonsense C.E.O.

of a gambling casino in Deadwood, South Dakota, into the stalwart protector, the solver of feminine trials and tribulations…in other words, pure mush.

And Mitch did care about Karla, for her sake, because she was a genuinely nice person, and for his own sake, for she was the best assistant he had ever employed.

He had made some progress with Karla after calming her down following Natalie's dramatic little scene. With some gentle probing—in between dwindling, hiccuping sobs—Mitch had learned that Karla was determined to have and keep her baby. Not for any leftover feelings for the father, because she had none, but simply because it was *her* baby.

A decision Mitch silently applauded.

Still, Karla had maintained that she felt too ashamed to go to her parents, who lived in Rapid City, to ask for their financial or moral support. Karla was an only child, so there were no siblings to apply to for assistance. And, though she had made some friends in the year and a half she had been in Deadwood, she felt none were close enough to dump her problems on.

That left him, Mitch Grainger, the man with the tough exterior, surrounding a core of marshmallow in regards to weeping, defenseless females.

Helluva note, for sure.

An ironic smile of acceptance teased the corners of his sculpted, masculine lips. He'd take on the combined roles of surrogate father, brother and friend to Karla because of his soft spot…and because, if he didn't, and his sister ever found out about it, she'd have his hide.

His humor restored, Mitch reached for the intercom to summon Karla, just as a timid rap sounded on his office door, followed by the subdued sound of Karla's voice.

"May I come in, Mr. Grainger?"

"Yes, of course." He sighed; despite the numerous times he had asked her to call him Mitch, Karla had persisted in the more formal address. Now, after the emotional scene enacted mere minutes before, the formality seemed ludicrous. "Come in and sit down," he instructed as the door opened and she stepped inside. "And, from now on, call me Mitch."

"Yes, sir," she said meekly, crossing to the chair in front of his desk and perching on the edge of the seat.

He threw his hands up in exasperation. "I

give up, call me anything you like. How are you feeling?''

"Better.'' She managed a tremulous smile. "Thank you…for the use of your shoulder to cry on.''

He smiled back. "I've had plenty of practice. Years back, my younger sister went through a period in her teens when she was a regular waterworks.'' His wry confidence achieved the desired effect.

She laughed and eased back in the chair. But her laughter quickly faded, erased by a frown of consternation. "About Miss Crane…I'd like to go see her, explain…''

"No.'' Mitch cut her off, his voice sharp.

Karla bit her trembling lip, blinked against a renewed well of tears. "But…it was a misunderstanding,'' she said, her voice unsteady. "Surely, if I talked to her…''

He silenced her with a slashing movement of his hand. "No, Karla. Natalie didn't ask for, or wait long enough to hear an explanation. She added one and one and came up with three— you, me and your baby. Her mistake.'' His tone hardened with cold finality. "It's over. Now, let's discuss another matter of business.''

She frowned. "What business?''

"Your business."

"Mine?" Karla's expression went blank.

"The baby," he said, nudging her memory. "Your baby. Have you made any plans? Do you want to keep working? Or..."

"Yes, I want to keep working," she interrupted him. "That is, if you don't mind?"

"Why would I mind?" He grinned. "Hell, you're the best assistant I've ever employed."

"Thank you." A pleased glow brightened her brown eyes, and a flush colored her pale cheeks.

"Okay, you want to continue working."

"Oh, yes, please."

"How long?"

"As long as I can." Karla hesitated a moment before quickly adding, "I'd like to work up to the last possible minute."

"Forget it." He shook his head. "I don't think that would be good for you or the baby."

"But the work's not really physical," she insisted. "Having a baby is expensive today, and I'll need every dollar I can earn."

"I provide excellent health insurance coverage for you, Karla," he reminded her. "Including maternity benefits."

"I know, and I appreciate that, but I want to save as much as I can for afterward," she explained. "I'll need enough to tide me over until I can go back to work."

"Don't concern yourself with finances, I'll take care of that. I want you to concentrate on taking care of yourself, and the child you're carrying." He held up a hand when she would have protested. "Five more months, Karla."

"Six," she dared to bargain. "I'll only be seven-and-a-half months by then."

He smiled at her show of temerity. "Okay, six," he conceded. "But you will spend that sixth month training your replacement."

"But it won't take me a whole month to train someone," she exclaimed. "I won't have anything to do!"

"Exactly. Consider it a small victory that I'm allowing that much."

She heaved a sigh of defeat. "You're the boss."

"I know." His grin lasted all of a few seconds before turning into a grimace. "Damn," he muttered. "When the time comes, how in the hell are we ever going to find someone suitable to replace you?"

A little over a month later, and many miles distant to the southeast, an individual ministorm raged beneath a sun-drenched corner of Pennsylvania....

"Rat." The scissors slashed through the voluminous skirt.

"Louse." A seam tore asunder.

"Jerk." The bodice was sheared into small pieces.

"Creep." Tiny buttons went flying.

"There...done." Her chest heaving from her emotion-driven exertions, Maggie Reynolds stepped back and glared down at the ragged shards of white watered taffeta material that had formerly been the most exquisite wedding gown she had ever seen.

With a final burst of furious energy, she gave a vicious kick of one bare foot, scattering the pile of material into large and small pieces that glimmered in the early June sunlight streaming through the bedroom window.

Tears pricked her eyes; Maggie told herself it was the glare of sunlight, and not the fact that she was to have been married in that designer extravagance in two weeks' time.

The sting in her eyes grew sharper. Just two days before, Maggie's intended groom had thrown her a vicious curveball right out of left field. After sharing her apartment and her bed with him for nearly a year, and after all the arrangements for their wedding had been in place for months, she had come home from work to find all of his belongings gone, his clothes closet empty, and a note—a damned note—propped against the napkin holder on the kitchen table. The words he had written were imprinted on her memory.

Maggie, I'm sorry, I really am, he had scrawled on the lined yellow paper she kept for grocery lists. *But I can't go through with our marriage. I have fallen in love with Ellen Bennethan, and we are eloping to Mexico today. Please try not to hate me too much. Todd.*

The thought of his name brought his image front and center in Maggie's mind. Average height, sharp dresser, attractive, with coal-black hair and pale blue eyes. And, evidently, a class-A cheat. A sneer curled her soft lips. Hate him? She didn't hate him. She despised him. So, he had fallen in love with Ellen Bennethan, had he? Bull. He had fallen in love with her money. Ellen, a meek, simpering twit, who had never worked a day in her life, was the only child and heir of Carl Bennethan, owner and head honcho of the Bennethan Furniture Company, and Todd's employer.

Dear Todd had just taken off, leaving Maggie to clean up the mess after him. Which in itself was bad enough. But the thing that bit the deepest was that they had made love the very night before he split.

No, Maggie corrected herself with disgust. They hadn't made love, they had had sex. And it hadn't been great sex, either. Great? Ha! It had never been great. Far from it. From the beginning, Todd had been less than an enthusiastic lover, never mind energetic.

Or was she the less-than-energetic one?

How many times over the previous year had she asked herself that question? Maggie mused, self-doubt raising its nasty little head in her mind. In truth, she acknowledged, she had never become so passionately aroused that she felt swept away by the moment. Perhaps there was something lacking in her....

The hell with that, Maggie thought, anger reasserting itself to overwhelm doubt. And, to hell with Todd, and men in general. In her private opinion, sex was highly overrated, a fictional fantasy.

Outrage restored, Maggie made a low growling sound deep in her throat, and gave the rendered sparkling white pieces another scattering kick.

"Bastard."

"Feel better now?"

Maggie spun around at the sound of the smoky, dryly voiced question, to glare at the young woman leaning with indolent nonchalance against the door frame. The woman, Maggie's best friend, Hannah Deturk, was tall, slim, elegant and almost too beautiful to be tolerated.

Maggie had often thought, and even more often said, that if she didn't like Hannah so much, she could easily and quite happily hate her.

"Not a hell of a lot," Maggie admitted in a near snarl. "But I'm not finished yet, either."

"Indeed?" Hannah raised perfectly arched honey-brown eyebrows. "You're going to take the scissors to your entire trousseau?"

"'Course not," Maggie snapped. "I'm neither that stupid nor that far gone."

"Could'a fooled me," Hannah drawled. "I'd say, any woman who'd tear apart a gorgeous three-thousand-dollar wedding gown in a fit of rampant rage is about as far gone as is possible for a woman to be."

Just as tall as her friend, just as slim, and no

slouch herself in the looks department, with her long mass of flaming-red hair and her creamy complexion, Maggie gave Hannah a superior look and a sugar-sweet smile.

"Indeed?" she mimicked. "Well, there's possible, and then there's possible. Stick around, friend, and I'll demonstrate possibilities that'll blow your mind."

"You almost scare me," Hannah said, a thread of concern woven through her husky voice. "But I will stick around...just to ensure you don't hurt yourself."

"I'm already hurt," Maggie cried, a rush of tears to her eyes threatening to douse the fire of anger in their emerald-green depths.

"I know." Hannah relinquished her pose in the doorway to go to Maggie. "I know," she murmured, drawing her friend into a protective embrace.

"I'm sorry, Hannah," Maggie muttered, sniffing. "I promised myself I wouldn't cry anymore."

"And you shouldn't," Hannah said, her voice made raspy with compassion. "That son of a bitch isn't worth the time of day from you, never mind your tears."

Maggie was so startled by Hannah's curse—

Hannah *never* cursed—she stepped back to stare at her friend in tear-drying amazement.

Hannah shrugged. "Occasionally, when I'm seriously upset or furious, I lose control of my mouth."

"Oh." Maggie blinked away the last of the moisture blurring her vision and swiped her hands over her wet cheeks. "Well, you must be seriously one or the other, because I've known you since soon after you arrived here in Philadelphia from flyover country, and this is the first time I've ever heard a swear word from you."

"Actually, I'm seriously both," Hannah drawled, her tone belying the glitter in her blue eyes. "It just fries me that you're tearing yourself apart over that...that...slimy, two-timing, money-grabbing slug."

"Thanks, friend," Maggie murmured, moved by Hannah's concern for her. "I appreciate your support."

"You're welcome." A smile curved Hannah's full lips. "And it's Nebraska."

"What?"

"The flyover country I come from is the State of Nebraska," she answered.

"Oh, yeah, I knew that," Maggie said, interest sparking in her green eyes. "What's it like there...in Nebraska?"

Hannah frowned, as if confused by both the question and her friend's sudden show of interest on a topic she'd never before evinced any curiosity over. "The section I came from? Mostly rural, kind of placid, and at the time I decided to move to the big city, I thought, pretty dull."

"Sounds like just the ticket," Maggie mused aloud in a contemplative mutter.

"Just the ticket," Hannah repeated in astonishment. "For what? Being bored silly? What are you getting at?"

Maggie's smile could only be described as reckless. "You know those possibilities I mentioned?"

"Ye-e-es…" Hannah eyed her with budding alarm. "But now I'm almost afraid to ask."

Maggie laughed; it felt good, so she laughed again. "I'll tell you, anyway. Come with me, my friend," she invited, turning away from the room and the scattered debris that had once been her wedding gown. "Venting my spleen in here made me thirsty. We'll talk over coffee."

"You can't be serious." Her half-full cup of coffee—her third—in front of her, Hannah stared at Maggie in sheer disbelief.

"I assure you I am. Dead serious," Maggie

said, her features set in lines of determination. "I have already started the ball rolling."

"By slashing your gown to ribbons?" Hannah asked, her tone reflecting the hope that her friend hadn't done something even more drastic.

"Oh, that. That was symbolic." Maggie dismissed the act with a flick of her hand. "I couldn't stand looking at it another minute. No," she said, shaking her head. "What I have done to get the ball rolling was to spend this lovely Sunday morning composing notes to all the guests invited to the wedding, informing them that there would be no wedding, after all, e-mailing those on-line, and preparing the rest for snail-mail delivery."

"If you'd given me a holler, I'd have gladly helped you with that," Hannah said, heaving a sigh of exasperation.

"Thanks, but, well..." Maggie shrugged. "That chore is done."

"You didn't e-mail your parents...." Hannah's eyebrows shot up. "Did you?"

"Well, of course not. I telephoned them." Maggie sighed. "They were understandably upset, insisted I go spend some time with them in Hawaii."

"Good idea."

Maggie gave a quick head shake. "No, it isn't. They both took early retirement and moved to Hawaii to relax after Dad's mild heart attack. If I went there, in the mood I'm in, Mom would probably knock herself out to fuss all over me. Dad would likewise fret, curtail his golf games and try to distract and entertain me. And I'd feel guilty as hell because of it."

Hannah frowned but nodded. "I suppose."

Maggie soldiered on. "I also drafted a letter to my superior at work, giving my one-month notice of my intention to leave the firm."

Hannah's eyes widened with alarm. "Maggie, you didn't."

"I did," Maggie assured her, raising a hand to keep her friend from interrupting. "What's more, I faxed a Realtor I know, asking him if he'd be interested in listing my apartment for sale."

Hannah jumped from her chair. "Maggie, no." She shook her head, setting her sleek, bobbed honey-brown hair swinging. "You can't do that."

"I damn well can," Maggie retorted. "My grandmother left this place to me, I own it free and clear." She rolled her eyes. "And the forever taxes that go with it."

"But…" Her hair swung again, wildly. "Why? Where will you go? Where will you live?"

"Why? Because I'm tired of the treadmill, nose to the grindstone, following the rules." Maggie shrugged. "Who knows, maybe I'll join the circus."

"I don't believe I'm hearing this." As if unable to remain still, Hannah began to pace back and forth in front of the table. "To give up your job, sell your apartment…" Hannah threw up her hands. "That's crazy."

"Hannah—" Maggie came close to shouting "—I feel crazy."

"So you're just going to take off?"

"Yes."

"For how long, for Pete's sake?"

Maggie hesitated, shrugged, then answered, "Until I'm broke, or no longer feel crazy enough to break things and hurt people…Todd what's-his-name in particular."

"Oh, Maggie," Hannah murmured in commiseration, dropping onto her chair. "He's not worth all this anguish."

"I know that," Maggie agreed. "But knowing it doesn't help. So I'm cutting out, cutting loose."

"But, Maggie…" Hannah actually wailed.

Maggie shook her head, hard. "You can't change my mind, Hannah. I've got the itch to run free for a while and I'm going to scratch it."

"But you must have some idea where you're going," Hannah persisted, always the one for detail.

"No." Maggie shrugged. "Who knows, maybe I'll wind up in Nebraska."

Two

Three months later

The redhead knocked the breath out of him. A jolt of energy, physical and sexual in nature, made the body-blow a double whammy.

Mitch was both shocked and confused by his reaction to the woman Karla ushered into his office. It certainly wasn't that she was a stunning beauty; she wasn't. Oh, it wasn't that she was not attractive; she most definitely was, very attractive. But he knew many attractive and even a few stunning women, and yet he had never experienced such a strong and immediate response to any one of them.

Strange.

Baffled, yet careful not to reveal his condition, Mitch studied the woman as she crossed the room to his desk. On closer inspection, one might even concede she possessed a particular beauty...if one had a weakness for tall, slender women with creamy skin, a wide mouth with full lips, slightly slanted forest-glen-green eyes and long, thick hair of a deep shade of flaming red.

Apparently, Mitch wryly concluded, he did have such a previously unrecognized weakness.

At least, his knees felt a little weak; he felt the tremor in them when she drew closer.

Up close, she looked even better...damn the luck.

But, one thing was for certain, Mitch mused, she sure as hell hadn't dressed to make an impression. Her casual attire made a silent declaration of her utter disregard for conventional, or his personal, opinion.

She came to a stop next to a chair in front of his desk.

Mitch came to his senses.

Cursing his uncharacteristic distraction, he made a show of perusing her application.

"Ms. Reynolds?" Raising his gaze from the papers in his hand, he offered her a faint smile.

"Yes." Her attractive voice was soft, modulated, neutral, her return smile a pale reflection of his own.

He leaned forward over his desk and extended his right hand. "Mitch Grainger," he said, amazed by the tingling sensation caused by the touch of her palm to his in the brief handshake. "Have a seat." He flicked the still-tingling hand at the chair beside her.

"Thank you." With what appeared to be relaxed and effortless grace, she stepped in front of the chair and lowered herself into it. Settled, she met his direct stare with calm patience.

Watch it, Grainger, Mitch advised himself. *This is one woman determined not to be intimidated.*

He arched a brow. "If you'll excuse me a moment, while I give your application a quick once-over?"

She deigned to nod her permission.

Cool? Mitch speculated, unlocking his gaze from the brilliant green of hers to skim the application. Or was she, like Natalie Crane, just plain glacier-cold, through and through?

To his astonishment, after the fiasco of his engagement, Mitch found himself anticipating the opportunity to discover the answers to his questions about this particular woman.

Speed-reading the forms, Mitch quickly concurred with Karla's enthusiastic opinion; Maggie Reynolds's credentials were very impressive. A fact that had been pleasing to them both as Karla had been thus far unsuccessful in finding a suitable replacement.

Lifting his head, Mitch tested her with a piercing stare and his most forbidding tones. "You can produce references to confirm the information provided?"

"Not at hand," she said, her voice as cool and unruffled as her demeanor. "But I can obtain them."

He nodded; he had expected no less. "You appear to be well qualified for this position," he admitted, unfamiliar excitement quickening inside him at the idea of her working for him, at his beck and call, five days a week. But his hidebound sense of honor insisted he be completely honest. "In fact, you are overqualified. A bigger city would offer you much better opportunities for corporate advancement.''

She smiled.

His blood pressure rose a notch.

''I'm aware of that,'' she said. ''But, while I appreciate your candor, and advice, I'll pass on it.''

Too cool, Mitch reiterated…and just a hint of condescension. The woman had guts to spare; not many dared to condescend to him.

''Why?'' He shot the question at her.

She didn't shoot back. Then again, maybe she did, only she fired with a flashing, mind-bending smile.

Mitch felt the hit…and rather enjoyed it.

''As I explained to your assistant, and as my application attests, I've been there, done that,'' she said. ''I'm tired of the struggle.'' She shrugged. ''I suppose you might say my edge got dull.''

Mitch wouldn't have said there was a damn thing dull about her. At any rate, he wasn't prepared to say it to her, not at this point of their association. And, for some reason, or quirk in his own nature, he was determined on their having an association.

''I see'' was all he would say.

"Besides," she continued, "I like the look of this town, the Old West ambience. It's quaint."

Quaint. Mitch nodded. It was that. "When did you arrive? Have you seen much of the town?" He had to smile. "Not that there's much to see."

"I…er, strolled around this morning," she answered, her hesitancy and obvious reluctance revealing her first signs of uncertainty.

Mitch decided to probe for the reason for her reticence. "You didn't take a ride on the Deadwood Trolley?"

She shook her head, setting her hair swaying around her shoulders like living flames…and kicking his imagination into high gear.

"No." Her full, tempting lips curved into a faint smile; his imagination soared off the gauge. "My father always said that shoe-leather express was the best way to see any city," she explained. "I can ride the trolley another day."

As fascinated as Mitch surely was by her mouth, he didn't miss the fact that she had answered only part of his two-part question. Naturally, he wondered why.

"And when did you say you arrived?" he asked, with gentle persistence.

A spark flared to life in the depths of her fab-

ulous green eyes. Annoyance, anger? Mitch
mused.

"I didn't say." Her voice held an edge.

Good, Mitch thought. He wanted her on edge,
off balance, her cool composure rattled. In his
experience, he had found he learned more that
way.

"I know." He smiled...and waited.

She sighed, clearly losing patience with his
persistence. "I arrived yesterday," she finally
admitted.

Mitch wasn't through yet. "From where?
Philadelphia?"

She gave him a level look, as if taking his
measure. Mitch felt that tingly sensation again,
this time throughout his entire system. He liked
it. Once more, he merely smiled and waited, returning her measuring look.

"No." She didn't smile; she met his look
with green fire. "I left Philly months ago, on an
extended vacation tour of the country. I arrived
here via a small town in Nebraska, where I had
stopped for lunch."

"But you were originally headed for Deadwood?" Mitch thought it a reasonable question.
Evidently, Ms. Maggie Reynolds did not, if her

fleeting expression of exasperation was anything to go by.

"No." She shook her head, setting the red strands swirling once more.

Mitch's fingers itched to delve into the fiery mass, just to see if it burned him. When she didn't continue on with an explanation, he raised a nudging eyebrow, determined now to hear the whole of her story.

Silence stretched between them for several seconds, then she capitulated with a the-hell-with-it shrug. "While waiting for my lunch, I checked my finances," she said grittily. "The bottom-line balance indicated that it was time for me to go back to work—" she shrugged "—and here I am."

She had managed to surprise him, a rare accomplishment for anyone; he had long since been surprised by much of anything. Mitch glanced down at the bona fides on her application. A frown creased his brow when he looked up at her. "I don't get it," he admitted. "With your credentials, you could have secured an excellent-paying position in any major city." He refrained from adding that he was glad she hadn't. "Why Deadwood?"

She shifted in her chair, revealing her mounting impatience. "I think I've already explained that."

He agreed with a slight nod. "Been there, done that, tired of the grind. Right?"

"Yes." Her smile had a hint of smugness.

"But, if you're running out of money..." Mitch let his voice trail off, not yet ready to let her off the hook by quoting the salary he was prepared to offer her, for he definitely was going to hire her.

"I'm not running out of money," she corrected him. "I'm running a bit low. There is a difference."

"Point taken," he admitted, deciding he liked this woman's style. "But...why Deadwood?" he repeated, now merely curious about her choice.

She smiled.

His stomach muscles constricted.

"Believe it or not," she said, "I overheard the men seated in the booth behind me talking about it." She shrugged. "So, I figured...why not?"

Guts, style and insouciance. Some combination, and, thankfully, not in the least similar to Natalie, Mitch thought, tamping down an urge to laugh. He was looking forward to working with, matching wits with and, hopefully, gaining a more intimate relationship with this woman. But he didn't want to appear too eager or show his hand too soon.

"As I'm sure you couldn't help but notice, my assistant is in her third trimester of pregnancy," he said.

"It is pretty hard to miss," she responded dryly.

"Yes." He paused, allowed his concern for Karla to show on his expression. "I'm growing anxious about finding someone to replace her, she needs to rest more." He paused again, pursed his lips, just for effect.

She didn't betray knowledge of his "effect." She held his steady gaze with cool green eyes.

His admiration for her expanding, Mitch silently applauded her display of composure. "That being the case, the position is yours...if you still want it."

"I do." She nodded. "Thank you."

Then he quoted a salary figure.

That got a reaction from her. It was quick, but there, in the slight flicker of surprise in her eyes, her expression. She controlled it just as quickly.

"That's more than generous," she said. "When would you like me to start?"

Immediately, he thought. "As soon as possible," he said.

"It's Thursday." She raised a perfectly arched, dark red eyebrow. "Will Monday suit?"

"Fine," he agreed, somehow certain it would be a very long weekend.

Although she had endured the actual torture rather than allow her consternation to show, Maggie exited Grainger's office feeling as if she had been grilled to a turn by the Spanish Inquisition. She recalled the conversation she had overheard last night in a nearby restaurant. A woman who had interviewed for this position had stated a very adept description of Mitch Grainger. That young woman in the restaurant hadn't exaggerated; he was every bit as hard as bedrock, maybe harder, hard and tough, intelligent and probing, and physically attractive... devastatingly so.

After that nerve-jangling interview, Maggie felt as if his image was imprinted on her mind, never to be erased. And the image was more than a little disturbing.

The first thing Maggie had noticed about Mitch Grainger, even as he sat behind his desk, was his height. He was tall, at least six two, possibly three. He had the lean, well-toned body of a top-notch, worth-a-bizillion-dollars quarterback. His hair was dark, his eyes a piercing gray. His skin was sun-burnished. His clothes were expensive, impeccably tailored to his broad-shouldered, long-muscled frame.

Yes, indeedy, Mitch Grainger was sexy and good-looking…if one were susceptible to sharply defined features, cool reserve, an air of absolute command, blatant sensuality and quick, intelligent wit with attitude.

Fortunately, for Maggie's peace of mind, she was not so inclined. Within seconds of entering his office, she had labeled him an arrogant, chauvinistic ram, hiding inside the trappings of civilized clothing.

And she had just signed on to work for the man. The emotional side of Maggie urged her to run for the nearest exit. Her practical side reminded her that she needed the money, or she wouldn't be running very far for very long.

"How did it go?" Karla asked, equal measures of anxiety and hope in her tones.

Jarred from her less-than-encouraging introspection, Maggie dredged up a smile. "He hired me. I start Monday."

As if she had been holding it, Karla's breath

came out in a whooshing sound. "Oh, good," she said, a bright smile lighting her pretty face. "He was driving me crazy."

Great. Just what she needed to hear, Maggie thought, sinking onto the chair Karla indicated with a wave of her hand. Convinced her initial concern about Karla's obvious anxiety over finding her replacement was because the man was an absolute tyrant, she was almost afraid to ask "Why?"

"He thinks I should rest more."

"So he said," Maggie confided.

"Oh, he's so-o-o protective," Karla said, heaving a sigh and rolling her eyes. "This last week especially...just because my ankles have been swelling a little."

He was so-o-o protective? He noticed a little swelling in her ankles? Well, she guessed she could credit the man's supposed tyrannical behavior as the reason for Karla's overanxiousness, Maggie thought, her mental gears beginning to spin.

Why would an employer, a bedrock-hard employer at that, evince such concern...her gears ground to a halt at a sudden, most startling of questions: could Mitch Grainger be the father of Karla's baby?

Well, of course he could, Maggie chided herself. He was a man, wasn't he? A blatantly sensuous man.

For some inexplicable reason beyond her comprehension, she suddenly felt queasy.

"Is something wrong?" Karla asked, peering at Maggie with concern. "You're pale. Are you feeling ill?"

No, not ill, disgusted, Maggie assured herself, working up another smile. "No..." She shook her head and raked her mind for a reasonable response. "I...er, everything happened so fast, you know. It's exciting but a little unnerving, too." She managed a laugh, a weak one, but a laugh. Sort of. "I mean, who ever expects to get hired for a job—" she snapped her fingers "—like that?"

"I know what you mean." Karla laughed, too, for real. "But that's Mr. Grainger's way. He is decisive, forceful, and he has a tendency to be a bit overwhelming."

A bit? Like a bulldozer. Maggie kept her opinion to herself. All she said, dryly and wryly, to Karla was "I noticed."

The other woman giggled. "I think I'm going to enjoy working with you for the next couple of weeks, Maggie, and—" she paused, suddenly looking very young and uncertain ''—I hope we can be friends.''

Maggie felt a tug at her heartstrings. Off the top of her head, she'd guess Karla to be twenty-two, maybe twenty-three, four or five years her junior. Yet the girl appeared so much younger, so vulnerable, she made Maggie feel old, if only in experience.

''I'm sure we will be,'' Maggie said, reaching across the desk to take Karla's hand. ''And, as a novice to the gambling business, I'm just as sure I'm going to need all the help you're willing to give me over the coming weeks.''

Fairly beaming, Karla squeezed Maggie's hand. ''With your experience, I'm positive you'll do fine.''

Yes, she would, Maggie silently agreed. That is, if she could tolerate the bulldozer. And it was a big if. But, first things first.

''I was hoping you also could help me with something else,'' she said.

''Of course, if I can,'' Karla said. ''What is it?''

''Well, right now, I've got a room at the Mineral Palace,'' she explained, her smile rueful. ''But I can't stay there. I need to find a place to rent, a furnished room or small apartment. I don't suppose you'd know of any?''

"Yes, I do, and it's right in my building!" Karla exclaimed, laughing. "And I can almost guarantee you'll be able to have it. It's a bachelor apartment. And it's fully furnished but…" She hesitated, frowned, bit her lip.

"But?" Maggie prompted, her burst of anticipation doing a nosedive.

"It's on the third floor and there's no elevator…would that be a problem?"

"Not at all," Maggie assured her, laughing in sheer relief. "Where's the apartment house located?"

"It's right outside of town, but it's not a regular apartment house," Karla explained. "A long time ago, it was a private residence, a large old Victorian house that's been renovated into apartments."

Although Maggie immediately envisioned a somewhat shabby old house with mere remnants of its former elegance, she told herself that beggars couldn't be choosers. Besides, she had always loved Victorian-style houses, even the ones that had seen better days. Deciding to accept circumstances as part and parcel of her crazy adventure, she smiled to set the still-frowning Karla at ease.

"Sounds interesting," she said, feeling re-

warded with the smile that chased the frown
from Karla's face.

"Who do I talk to about seeing the place?"

Karla's smile grew into a grin. "The boss."

"The boss?" Maggie's stomach rebelled.
"Mr. Grainger owns the building?"

"Yep." Karla nodded. "At least, his family
does," she qualified. "His great-great grandfather built the house…oh, somewhere around the
turn of the century, I think. It was several years
after he had established his bank here and married the daughter of one of the partners or man-
agers or executives or whatever of the Home-
stake gold mine."

"They own the bank, too?"

"No." Karla shook her head and frowned.
"The way I understand it, Mitch's great-
grandfather sold out the business in the twenties,
when he got into buying real estate. Then the
bank went under when the market crashed. Apparently, it was the land holdings that kept the
family from ruin during the depression, for they
managed to hang on to everything."

"Including the house that's now an apartment," Maggie inserted.

Karla nodded. "And this property." She
waved a hand, indicating the casino building.
"Both of which are under Mitch's control."

Wonderful. Maggie was hard-pressed to keep from groaning aloud. What to do? she asked herself, reluctant to go back into Mr. Grainger's office. While living in the same building as Karla would be nice, Maggie wasn't sure she wanted to both work for and rent from her employer. Besides, if her suspicions about Karla and him having an affair were correct, even though they somehow didn't seem to fit together, the idea of being around to witness their ''togetherness'' didn't appeal to Maggie in the least. And yet, she needed a permanent address, the sooner the better.

''I'll go talk to Mitch now,'' Karla said, settling the matter for Maggie by pushing herself out of her chair and turning to tap on his door.

Maggie opened her mouth to ask Karla to wait a moment, but before she could utter a sound, Karla had opened the door and slipped inside the office.

To her surprise, Maggie didn't have time to fume or to fidget, for within minutes, Karla was back, a triumphant smile on her face. She raised her hand to display a key clipped to a case dangling from her fingers.

''We're outta here,'' she said, motioning for Maggie to follow her as she skirted the desk and moved toward the outer hallway.

"But…" Maggie began.

"He gave me the rest of the afternoon off," Karla cut in breezily. "He told me to take his truck to run you out to have a look at the apartment. I'm to call him from there. If you like the place, I'm to use the truck to help you move your stuff…if you need help."

His truck? Frowning, Maggie scrambled out of her chair to hurry after the surprisingly agile woman. Should Karla be driving a truck in her advanced pregnancy? Never having been pregnant, she didn't have a clue.

They didn't go through the casino to the front entrance. Instead, at the base of the narrow stairway that led to the second floor, Karla turned to traverse another narrow hallway, leading to a steel door at the rear of the building. A burly uniformed guard stood posted next to the door.

"Hi, Karla, late lunch?" The guard smiled and gave Maggie a curious once-over.

"No." Karla grinned and shook her head. "The boss gave me the afternoon off." She turned to smile at Maggie. "Maggie, this is Johnny Brandon."

"Mr. Brandon," Maggie said, extending her right hand to be swallowed up in his.

Karla switched her glance back at the guard.

"Johnny, this is Maggie Reynolds. She'll be working here starting Monday."

"Pleased to meet you, Ms. Reynolds...and please, call me Johnny." The guard gripped her hand for a second, inclined his head, then shot a grin at Karla. "You've finally found someone to suit Mr. Grainger, huh?"

"Yes." Karla heaved a dramatic sigh, but ruined the effect with a giggle. "Finally. And now we're outta here, before he changes his mind about the afternoon off."

Chuckling, Johnny moved to open the door for them. "I can't see that happening. Nice to meet you, Ms. Reynolds."

"Maggie, please," she said, smiling as she followed Karla from the casino.

The exit led directly onto a parking lot. Trailing Karla, Maggie glanced around at the number of trucks parked in neatly aligned rows. The vehicle Karla stopped next to was not what Maggie had envisioned as a "truck," but a large dusty sports utility vehicle. But what a sports utility vehicle. Even with the coat of dust, the black behemoth fairly shouted *expensive*.

"Isn't it super?" Karla said, smiling at what Maggie knew must have been her bemused expression.

"And big," Maggie said, nodding. "No, huge."

Karla shrugged, and pushed a button on the key case, unlocking the doors. "These vehicles are almost a necessity in this mountainous terrain."

"What does it get, five miles to the gallon?" Circling the monster, Maggie slipped into the plush passenger seat, noting that plush described the entire interior.

"A little more than that," Karla said, grinning as she carefully slid behind the wheel. "But it drives like a dream," she continued, giving evidence that she had driven the vehicle before. "Like a luxury car, really." Firing the engine, she proved the claim by smoothly maneuvering the purring beast out of the parking lot.

"You know, I really don't need help moving my stuff, if I decide to take the apartment. We wouldn't have had to waste Mr. Grainger's fuel." Maggie turned her head to smile at Karla. "We could have used your car."

"No, we couldn't," Karla said, laughing. "Because I don't have a car."

"Then how do you get around—to shop, to work?" Maggie asked. "Is the house within walking distance?"

"Well I have walked, and I still could, if I

wanted, which I don't, at least not anymore.''
Karla smiled and shook her head. ''No, Mitch
drives me in to work.''

Uh-huh, Maggie thought, growing more convinced about an intimate relationship between
the two. Unbidden, and shocking, a vision rose
in her mind of the bedrock-hard Mitch Grainger
and the soft, puppy-friendly Karla, locked and
writhing in a lovers' embrace. She immediately
blanked the image. For some strange, confusing
reason, she felt upset, almost hurt by the very
thought of him making love to Karla.

Another thought rushed in, nearly as upsetting
as the first, a horrifying thought that required
immediate clarification.

''Does Mr. Grainger live in the house?'' she
asked, hearing the ragged threads of strain in her
voice.

''Oh, no,'' Karla answered. ''He has an apartment on the third floor of the casino, above the
office.''

Relief washed through Maggie, only to be followed by an odd and unwelcome sense of de-
jection at this further proof of their relationship.
Why else, she reasoned, would he put himself
out to fetch Karla back and forth?

Three

The house was beautiful.

Maggie fell in love with it on sight. It reminded her of the lovely old Victorian houses that had been converted into bed-and-breakfast inns in Cape May, New Jersey. But this house had been built on an even grander scale, and was a true mansion. It had a deep-roofed wraparound porch, intricate and lacy-looking decorative gingerbread and a copper-roofed tower on one corner.

Gazing up at the distinctive bell-shaped roof, Maggie quivered with anticipation at the realization that there were windowed tower alcoves on all three floors of the building. Having lived all her life in modern, boxlike apartments, first with her parents, then in the similar flat her grandmother had willed to her, Maggie loved old-fashioned places with nooks and crannies.

"So, what do you think?" Karla asked, breaking into Maggie's bemused near-trance.

"It's…magnificent," Maggie murmured.

"Big, too." Karla laughed. "Do you want to come in, or just stand here and stare at the outside of the place?"

"I want to come in," Maggie answered, grinning. "I can't wait to see the inside."

On entering the foyer, Maggie felt a pang of disappointment at the obvious but necessary changes that had been made to convert the once-gracious private home into apartments. Still, quite a bit of the former beauty remained in the original woodwork, including the hardwood flooring and the wide staircase attached to one wall. A hallway ran next to the stairway to the rear of the enormous house.

"As you can see, it wasn't at all difficult to section off for separate living accommodations," Karla said, motioning to the closed doors facing each other across the foyer. "This is my apartment.'' She moved to the door set into the stairway wall and inserted a key in the lock. ''Come on in.''

''Oh, you do have a tower alcove,'' Maggie said, eagerly following the younger woman. Once inside, she caught her breath on a soft ''Oh...it's beautiful, like stepping back in time.''

''Yes. I love it.'' Karla smiled.

''I can see why.'' Glancing around the generous-size living room, Maggie feasted her eyes on the period furniture and the curved, deeply padded window seat in the alcove.

The Victorian motif was carried through the rest of the apartment, even the small bathroom. Karla led the way into the kitchen at the back of the house. There, everything was bright with ultramodern white appliances.

''This room was originally the pantry and laundry room,'' Karla explained, moving to the sink. ''Would you like a cup of coffee or tea?''

''I'd love a cup of coffee,'' Maggie said, then qualified, ''But could I see the third-floor apartment first?''

Karla laughed. ''Of course you can see it.'' Turning, she led the way back into the living room. ''You might want to go on ahead,'' she said, grinning as she opened the door. "I'm a little slow lately going up the stairs."

Maggie's gaze rested on Karla's extended belly. "You don't have to go upstairs. I can go up alone. That is, if it's all right?"

"Oh, sure it's all right." Taking a key off the case Mitch had given her, Karla handed it to Maggie. "When you get to the top of the stairs, follow the hallway to the door at the back. Oh, and by the way, there's another enclosed staircase at the rear of the hallway, with an access door to the back parking area. I'll start the coffee while you have a look at the place."

At the second-floor landing Maggie found the door to the stairway leading to the third level. It was also enclosed, much narrower, but lit by a ceiling light and by the sunlight pouring in through lacy curtains at a window at the top landing.

Not knowing what to expect...a big old storage attic, or perhaps a large room sectioned off for servants' quarters, Maggie mounted the stairs. A wide hallway with sloping ceilings to either side ran to an enlarged room at the front. While she had expected the sloping roofs, she hadn't expected the storage cabinets built into the spaces beneath—nooks and crannies—or the size of the apartment beyond.

It was spotlessly clean, huge and wonderful and completely furnished, again with the same Victorian motif. To one side, the bedroom and bath were both sectioned off and private. To the other side one large room made up the kitchen and living area. A small round dinette table sat in the tower alcove, and a lace-curtained window overlooked the front of the house.

A strange sense of excitement stirred inside Maggie, a feeling almost as if she had found exactly what she had spent months unknowingly searching for.

A home…or a hideaway? Maggie didn't know, nor did she care. It felt right, and that was enough, enough even to put up with the bedrock-hard Mitch Grainger.

Picturing herself seated at the table, gazing out at the world while eating a meal, sipping a cup of hot chocolate on a cold night or a glass of iced tea on a hot afternoon, Maggie decided on the spot that she had to have the apartment, regardless of cost, or her new employer. With the salary figure he had quoted, she knew she could afford it, even though she had immediately thought of finding an inexpensive place and hoarding most of her money away.

Oh, well, she mused, slowly looking around, already feeling at home. She had to have it, and that was that.

Anxious to lay claim to it and move in her things, she gave a final longing glance at the alcove, then retraced her steps down to the ground level.

As promised, Karla had the coffee ready, along with a plate of packaged cookies.

"So, what did you think of it?" Karla asked, nibbling on a cream-filled sandwich cookie.

"I love it. I want it," Maggie answered, taking a careful sip of the hot liquid. "How much?"

Karla shrugged. "I don't know." She popped the last morsel of cookie into her mouth, chewed and swallowed. "You'll have to take that up with Mitch." She reached for another cookie, paused, sighed and pulled back her hand. "Better not." She sighed again. "I love sweets, but at my last doctor visit, I had put on five pounds. The doctor was not happy." She grinned. "She told me to lay off the junk."

"Must be rough when you have a sweet tooth," Maggie commiserated. "I don't, never did.'' She rolled her eyes. ''My downfall is pasta…with rich sauces.''

''Really?'' Karla laughed. ''I was planning to make a pasta dish for dinner. Why don't we move your stuff as soon as we're finished here, then have dinner together?''

Maggie frowned. ''Are you sure Mr. Grainger won't mind if I move in before paying the rent?''

''I told you he said I should use the truck to help you move your stuff,'' Karla reminded her.

''Well…all right. But I have a better idea,'' Maggie countered, mindful of Karla's condition. ''Most of my stuff is still in my car, as I only took two cases into the hotel and didn't even fully unpack them. If you'll run me into town, I'll grab my cases, check out of the hotel and follow you back here. Then you can rest, put up your feet, while I lug my stuff up to the third floor.''

''Oh, brother, I'm not an invalid,'' Karla protested. ''You sound just like Mitch.''

''God, I hope not,'' Maggie said fervently.

Karla giggled. ''He's really quite nice, you know.''

''Uh-huh,'' Maggie muttered, reserving her opinion and judgment. ''Anyway, I have eyes,

and I couldn't help but notice your swollen ankles," she continued, deliberately changing the
subject. "So, instead of your standing at the
stove and cooking, when I'm finished lugging
my stuff, I'd like to thank you for all your help
by treating you to dinner at the restaurant of
your choice."

"But..."

"No buts," Maggie said, cutting her off.
"That's the deal." She grinned. "Take it or
leave it."

Karla threw up her arms. "You win." She
grinned back. "I'll take it."

"Good." Maggie shoved back her chair.
"Then let's clear away the coffee things and get
this show on the road."

The running and lugging were completed in
less than two hours. Of course, Maggie didn't
put a thing away, but simply dumped her four
suitcases, a nylon carry-on and one cardboard
carton in the middle of the living room. She did
take a minute to retrieve her makeup case,
though. Zipping into the bathroom, she fresh-
ened up, brushed her hair and swiped blusher on
her cheeks and lipstick on her lips before dash-
ing back down the stairs to collect Karla.

"Oh, I talked to Mitch on the phone while

you were carting your stuff upstairs,'' Karla said as they left the house. "He said you can take care of the rent payment on Monday morning, when you come in to work.''

"Fine." Maggie masked a grimace with a smile, not wanting to reveal to the friendly and obviously trusting young woman how reluctant she was to face Monday morning, and working for Mitch Grainger.

The next three days flew by in a flurry of domestic activity for Maggie. For the first time since leaving Philadelphia, she actually unpacked every one of her suitcases, the nylon flight bag and the cardboard carton. She stashed foldables into the drawers of an old-but-solid and highly polished wood dresser and, after a brisk shake-out, hung suits, dresses, skirts, slacks and blouses in the roomy bedroom closet.

A soft smile on her lips, Maggie arranged the top of the dresser with the few personal items she hadn't been able to leave behind: a framed enlarged snapshot of her parents; a small hand-carved jewelry box; the white jade figurine of a tiger that had been the last Christmas gift she'd received from her grandmother; and a small, stuffed, gaily garbed clown Hannah had presented to her as a going-away present.

Deciding to pick up some groceries, Maggie headed downstairs and out to her car. Once in the parking area, she turned to glance back at the house. A soft 'oh' of pleasure whispered through her lips as she took in the beauty of the house once more.

Utterly charmed by the sight of the grand old house, Maggie didn't allow herself to so much as conjecture on the possible length of her stay in Deadwood. She'd been hired to stay until Karla was able to return to work—some four or five months from now. Perhaps she would stay on a little longer, to experience more of the changing seasons in this part of the country.

But that would depend a lot on Mitch Grainger, Maggie reasoned, suppressing a sudden shiver of indeterminate origin. Why the mere thought of the man should so affect her, she hadn't a clue. Yet, whenever he came to mind, or Karla mentioned him, a chill trickled the length of her spine.

And he came to mind often throughout the weekend, too often for Maggie's peace of mind. At odd, disconcerting moments, an image of him, in full detail and living color, invaded her consciousness. Primarily when she was in bed.

All of a sudden, he'd be there, filling her mind, her senses. She'd experience the weird sensation that she could actually *feel* him, was as aware of him as she had been in his office. She could almost feel the compelling pull of his intent gray eyes, the sensual energy that surrounded him like a magnetic force field.

It was really the strangest sensation, one she had never experienced before, and she didn't like it. The sensation unnerved her, made her feel chilled, then too warm, tingly and quivery all over.

In a bid to dispel her uneasiness about working closely with him, Maggie conjured defensive images of Todd and every other man she had ever come into contact with who had come on to her.

Her ploy didn't work; those other images left her completely unaffected. Only the image of Mitch Grainger had the power to make her heart race, her breathing shallow, her nerves twang, as if his long fingers plucked them like guitar strings.

It was all just too ridiculous, Maggie repeatedly chastised herself, firmly, if unconsciously, entrenched in denial about the root cause of her awareness of him. Still, deep down inside, she knew the energy was sexual, the attraction mutual.

By bedtime Sunday night, to Maggie's way of thinking, those three days had elapsed much too quickly.

Four

For Mitch, those days dragged much too slowly.

Like an animal's instinctive restlessness before an approaching storm, Mitch felt an inner expectancy, as if something momentous was about to happen. He felt charged, wired, restless, and the feelings were centered around one Maggie Reynolds.

It was the damnedest sensation, unlike anything Mitch had ever felt before in connection to any woman. It bothered him to the point where it interfered with his concentration on his work, and that bothered him even more.

What was it about this particular woman? Mitch asked himself at least two dozen times during those seemingly endless three days.

Unlike his former fiancée, with her near-perfect, symmetrical features, Maggie Reynolds was decidedly not a classical beauty, he continually reminded himself. Yeah, yeah, Maggie was striking, with that tall, slender but curvaceous body, that mass of red hair, those flashing green eyes, those full kiss-me-if-you-dare lips.

Well, Mitch dared, but why the hell should he want to? he wondered, too often. Yes, she was bright, and quick, and cool…oh, so cool.

And yet, her coolness of manner was different from the remote and off-putting detachment that had been integral to Natalie's personality.

In Maggie, Mitch sensed a coolness based on confidence, not instilled by growing up rich and pampered, but earned by intelligence and competence.

But Mitch instinctively felt there was even more to it than that. There was a wariness within the depths of Maggie's cool green eyes that spoke of something, he suspected, having to do with men in particular, and not simply reserve or even arrogance. What that something might be teased and tantalized him.

So then, a challenge? Was that her unusual appeal?

Mitch spent an inordinate amount of time mulling that one over. It was possible, he conceded, since a sense of challenge in regards to a woman was a new and novel emotion for him. By and large, Mitch knew he was rather blasé so far as women were concerned, simply because he had never had to go out of his way to attract any woman he had ever shown the slightest interest in, as well as those he had not.

But Maggie Reynolds was different. She had revealed not the slightest interest in him, nor so much as a hint of feeling a bit intimidated by him.

An image of Maggie slipped in and out of his mind at unexpected, inconvenient intervals. Always the same, the image of her was as she had looked while seated across the width of his desk from him. And she had looked anything but a nervous supplicant, anxious about an interview for the employment position she obviously needed.

The picture of self-containment and confidence, Maggie had met and maintained his deliberate and steady regard with a cool composure bordering on detachment.

A challenge? Oh, yeah, Mitch concluded. Maggie Reynolds presented a challenge he couldn't wait to accept.

By Sunday evening, the sensation of simmering expectancy inside Mitch had ratcheted up to rioting anticipation. Unused to the unfamiliar feelings, he prowled the confines of his spacious apartment two floors above the casino, disgusted and amused in turn by the novel, disruptive emotional, physical and mental effect of the inner heightened eagerness.

It was a relief when his private phone line rang, simply because of its distraction value. Mitch snatched up the receiver on the second ring. The sound of his brother's voice centered his attention.

"How are you, ole son?" Justin drawled in his usual low, sardonic tones.

"Compared to whom?" Mitch drawled back, a warm smile curving his lips and coloring his voice.

Justin chuckled. "Me, for one."

Despite his brother's soft laughter, Mitch frowned with sudden concern. "There's something wrong with you?"

"Now, Mitch, don't go tying your guts into

protective big-brother knots,'' Justin said. "I'm fine.''

Mitch snorted at the big-brother reference. Less than two years separated them. But he was protective, he acknowledged. He always had been, not only of Justin and their sister, Beth, the baby of the brood, but of Adam, the eldest, who was even more protective of the rest of them. Come to that, a tightly knit group of four—rowdy angels, as their mother had lovingly called them—they were all protective of one another.

"But I do have a problem,'' Justin continued, "and I need a favor.''

"Name it,'' Mitch said at once. "What's the problem?''

"It's Ben.''

"Daniels? He isn't working out at the ranch?'' Mitch asked in surprise.

Though the varied business enterprises of the Grainger Corporation had been headed by Adam since their father's retirement, Mitch still kept tabs on everything concerning his family. He knew full well the story of Ben Daniels. It had begun the year he turned twenty-two, two years before he had been given control of the Deadwood casino.

Thirteen years before, Ben, a seventeen-year-old orphan, had hired on as a wrangler on the Grainger homestead in Wyoming, where Mitch and his siblings had been born and raised. All of the Graingers, from Mitch's father and mother, straight down the line of the kids, even Beth, who was three years younger, had taken the tall, lanky Ben under their protective wings.

Over the years Ben had developed a real ability for handling horses. Although he wasn't to the level of Justin, whose talent with horses was damn near uncanny, Ben had a solid working ability.

As he matured, Ben's good looks formed into sheer masculine handsomeness, and he was hell with the women. Three years ago, the eighteen-year-old daughter of an influential banker became pregnant and named Ben as the father. Ben denied it, claiming he had never been intimate with the girl, and insisted on a DNA study. It never came to that for, distraught and terrified of her father, the girl had swallowed a lethal dose of her mother's sleeping pills.

The traumatic incident had nearly destroyed Ben. Depressed, he began drinking, heavily. Afraid he'd wind up destroying himself, Adam had fired him from the homestead ranch, then rehired and relocated him to the Montana horse spread Justin managed for the family.

But that had all happened three years before, and Mitch had believed Ben had overcome his depression.

"That's the problem," Justin said, breaking in to Mitch's surprised ruminations. "He's working out too well. Damned man don't quit."

"And that's a problem?" Mitch asked, thinking he should have that problem with—thankfully—a few of his less-ambitious employees.

"Hell, yes, it's a problem," Justin said. "At least in Ben's case it is. He goes nonstop, seven days a week, from before dawn until after nightfall. I don't think he's been off the ranch more than five times in the three years he's been here. You..."

"Just about the same could be said about you," Mitch cut in to observe about the brother who had always been something of a loner, but even more so after the breakup of his early, ill-fated marriage. "How long has it been since you left the ranch, had a vacation?"

"It's my place, Mitch, my home, even if it is a part of the family business," Justin retorted. "Besides, not that it's any of your business," he added in a one-upmanship tone, "but I took a short vacation last week, spent some time in Wyoming with big brother Adam, his gorgeous bride Sunny and our adorable niece Becky.''

A soft smile softened Mitch's lips at the mention of the two-month-old baby; Becky *was* adorable. ''I took a quick trip down week before last,'' he said, laughing. ''I'm afraid ole Adam is in for a time of it in about fifteen or so years, because our Miss Becky is going to be a beauty.''

''Yeah,'' Justin concurred softly. ''Anyway, you should see Ben. He's honed down to nothing but muscle and bone. The man needs a break.''

''So, give him one,'' Mitch said. ''Tell him to take a vacation, get a little R and R.''

''I did.'' Justin sighed. ''He refused at first, but I made it an order and he finally agreed. That's where the favor from you comes in. Can you arrange a hotel room for him?''

''He's coming to Deadwood?''

''Yeah. Said if he's got to take a damn vacation, he may as well go there, hang out with you a little when you can spare the time, and lose some of the money he's stashed away over these past three years.''

"If he's hell-bent on losing his money, why not go to Vegas, then?"

Justin grunted. "Ben said it's too crowded, too high-tech and too glitzy."

"He's got a point," Mitch conceded.

"So, can you arrange a room, say at the Bullock Hotel, on short notice?"

"Sure." Mitch hesitated. "How short?"

"He's leaving tomorrow morning, should arrive late afternoon or early evening."

Mitch shook his head. "That is short notice. Why did you wait so long to call me?"

Justin laughed. "I laid the law down just a half hour ago. Ben was not happy."

"Tough." Mitch laughed with him. "I'll see what I can do about the Bullock."

"Thanks. Ben'll contact you when he gets in."

They talked for several more minutes, discussing family business, ranching business, casino business.

"Oh, and Mitch, keep an eye on Ben for me. He seems okay now, but I'd hate to see him go off the rails again," Justin said before hanging up.

Wonderful, Mitch thought, frowning at the dead phone receiver. Now he was to play keeper to a thirty-year-old man. Thinking the role had better not interfere with his plans for Maggie Reynolds, he disconnected, punched in the number for the Bullock and secured a room for Ben without a problem.

Maggie drove Karla to work on Monday morning, as prearranged with Mitch Grainger when he drove Karla home from work the previous Friday afternoon.

Maggie and Karla had spent so much of the weekend together, their budding friendship had truly blossomed. Which was fortunate, Maggie figured, as her stream of chatter during the drive could be attributed to the easy camaraderie they now shared.

The nervy, almost queasy feeling had been incrementally growing inside Maggie with each passing day until, this morning, she couldn't seem to shut up.

"Are you feeling all right?"

Well, so much for the cover of easy camaraderie, Maggie thought, slanting a quick glance at Karla and seeing her quizzical expression of concern.

"Oh, sure, I'm fine," Maggie answered, in forced tones meant to reassure. "I guess I'm a bit nervous.'' A bit? Try a bunch, she thought, swallowing an anxiety-induced bubble of self-derisive laughter.

Karla's look of concern gave way to a smile. ''I suppose that's understandable, with starting a new job,'' she said. ''But, trust me, as I told you before, there's really nothing to be nervous about.''

Trusting Karla was easy, Maggie thought, managing a smile for the cheery woman. During their gabfest over the weekend, Karla had been open and candid about herself, her life, even her reasons for not telling her parents about her pregnancy. She'd been open about everything—with one exception. Not once had Karla mentioned the circumstances surrounding her pregnancy, or the man who had fathered the child growing inside her.

So, of course, in light of Maggie's suspicions as to the identity of that man, and that tingly, almost electrifying sensation she had experienced while in his company, it was trusting Mitch Grainger she had doubts about. The troubling thing was, she didn't have anything concrete on which to place any of those doubts. All she had were her feelings, the vibes her senses had picked up while she had been in his office.

Her senses might have been wrong.

Yeah, and she might win a million-dollar lottery.

Maggie sighed as she pulled onto the employee parking lot. Crunch time. She'd soon know if she had been wrong, at least so far as that charged atmosphere was concerned.

"The first day's always the hardest," Karla said as she opened the outer office door. "So, the sooner we get started, the sooner it'll be over."

"Makes sense to me," Maggie agreed, catching the scent of fresh-brewed coffee as she followed Karla into the room. She'd skipped breakfast, and coffee, to allow herself more time to choose just the right clothes to wear—she'd tried on and discarded three perfectly suitable outfits before settling on a favorite skirt suit. The distinctive aroma of coffee set Maggie's senses clamoring for a strong dose of caffeine.

Alas, it was not to be. Karla sent them crashing with the information that, not only had their esteemed employer started the coffee—a cause for speculation in itself—it was decaf.

"Sorry," Karla said, her smile rueful. "But Mitch insisted we switch to decaffeinated after I told him I was pregnant...he said the caffeine was bad for the baby.''

Uh-huh, Maggie mused, her suspicions deepening. But she smiled and shrugged. "No problem," she said. "It wouldn't hurt me to cut down on the caffeine, either." Other than to further irritate nerves already jangling like discordant bells.

"Have a cup," Karla invited as she headed for the door to the inner office. "And a pastry." A wave of her hand indicated a selection of Danish pastries and sweet rolls arrayed on a tray next to the coffeemaker.

Mouth watering, stomach rumbling, Maggie was perusing the goodies on the tray when she heard Karla tap on the door and speak to "the boss."

Mitch knew the minute Karla and Maggie entered the outer office. He knew because he had planned it that way, by leaving his own office door open a crack.

Karla and Maggie were chatting. Mitch caught Karla say something about the first day being the hardest. The statement was certainly true in his case: it was his first day with Maggie in the office, and he was already getting hard.

Damn fool, Mitch cursed himself, disgusted with his body's immediate response to the muted sound of her voice, the mere idea of her presence. It had been years, long years, since his body had broken free of his mental control.

Sitting still, Mitch blanked out the chatter from the other room and drew slow, deep breaths, exerting his considerable willpower over his physical reaction. It required a lot of deep breaths, but he won the battle.

And not a moment too soon, for he had just returned his attention to the printout sheet on his desk when Karla tapped against his door and pushed it open another inch.

"Ready for coffee, Mitch?" she asked.

"Yes, Karla. Thank you."

Mitch was beginning to absorb the data on the sheet when Karla entered the room. He raised his head to smile and again thank her, only it wasn't Karla, it was Maggie crossing to his desk, a steaming cup in her hand.

"Good morning," he greeted her, slightly amazed by the cool, even tenor of his voice, considering the zing of intense awareness that shot through him.

This morning, Maggie definitely had dressed to impress; at least, her appearance impressed him. Her glorious mass of red hair had been tamed, smoothed back, away from her face. Her pin-striped navy suit was businesslike and smart, the jacket tailored, the skirt not too short, not too long. Beneath it she wore... What? All Mitch could see in the open vee of her buttoned jacket was skin, pale skin, as soft and creamy-looking as her face.

He was nearly undone by the sight of her.

"Good morning." She smiled.

Mitch had to fight against the urge to jump from his chair, leap over the desk, take her in his arms and claim her smile with his mouth.

Craziness. Pure craziness.

"Where do you want this?"

"Wherever." Coming to his senses, he motioned for her to set the cup anywhere on the desktop.

Maggie bent to set the cup near to hand and Mitch caught a brief glimpse of the shadowed valley between her breasts revealed by the slight gap in the jacket lapels.

Moisture rushed to his mouth. Heat pooled in his loins. Mitch told himself he was in big trouble.

"Will there be anything else, sir?" Her voice was too cool, too composed. It rankled him.

"Mitch," he said with firm determination, wanting to hear his name from her lips.

She blinked...with patently contrived surprise. "I beg your pardon?"

Sure you do, Mitch thought, feeling that exciting sense of challenge surge through him.

"I prefer working on a first-name basis... Maggie."

"But...I...I just started today," she said, as if that said it all.

Mitch cocked an eyebrow. "Your name will change tomorrow, or the next day, or next week?"

"Of course not." Her gorgeous green eyes glittered, shot fiery sparks at him.

Mitch loved it. "Neither will mine," he pointed out in tones designed to add fuel to her fire. "You'll still be Maggie. I'll still be Mitch."

She narrowed her eyes. He fought an impulsive bark of laughter. Oh, yeah, they were going to clash, and he was going to enjoy every minute of it.

"If you insist...Mitch," she said through gritted, sparkling white teeth.

His name from her lips hadn't had quite the sound he had wanted to hear, but, hey, Mitch told himself, anything was better than nothing.

Any concession from her, however slight and reluctantly given, was a win.

"I do insist," he drawled, wondering at the excitement shimmering through him over what was in reality such an inconsequential exchange.

She heaved a sigh, conveying impatience. The deliberate action lifted her breasts into prominence…and Mitch's excitement level to uncomfortable heights. He swallowed a groan of combined frustration and self-ridicule.

Never, never had he experienced anything remotely similar to the feelings this woman so effortlessly stirred in him. It was damned annoying.

"Will there be anything else?" she repeated, minus the formal address, and his name.

"Just one other thing," he said, plucking another sheet of paper from beneath the printout. "I faxed your former employer Friday for confirmation of your references." He glanced down at the piece of paper. "I received this faxed reply less than an hour ago."

"And?" she asked.

Leaning back in his chair, Mitch raised his head to meet her steady, confident regard. "Confirmation in spades," he said. "One might even say a rave review."

Maggie inclined her head. "Thank you." Though her tone was even, bare of so much as a hint of smugness, her eyes glittered with the gleam of justification.

Mitch allowed her the moment of self-satisfaction, for he had harbored some doubt about the veracity of her credentials, and the verification of them proved she had earned it. Then, the moment over, he moved his hand, just enough to rattle the paper, and threw her a curve.

"Along with the superlatives, your former employer expressed his disappointment, surprise and bafflement at your sudden decision to leave the company." Watching her closely for any reaction, he caught the slight stiffening of her body, the quick alertness in her eyes. "I must confess to my own share of curiosity as to your reasons."

"I believe I've already explained," Maggie said, her voice tight, militant.

"Ah, yes," Mitch murmured, thrilling to the green glare of challenge in her eyes. "Been there, done that."

"Yes." Her reply came close to a hiss.

There was more to it than that. Mitch knew it as sure as he knew that winter brought snow to the Dakotas. Too much time had elapsed between the date she had left Philadelphia and when she had arrived in Deadwood. His gut feeling was that Maggie was on the run from something…or someone. He opted for the someone, and that the someone was a man.

"Will there be anything else…Mitch?" she repeated for the third time, her tone now hard, her eyes as sharp as shards of green glass.

Cancel any doubts, Mitch thought. It had to have been a man. If it were anything else, something unsavory or illegal, Maggie would be on the defensive, but she wasn't. Just the opposite, in fact. Maggie was quick to go on the offensive, cool, collected and defiant.

Magnificent.

While Mitch itched to plumb the depths of her defiance, he decided to give her a break and back off for a spell. Besides, if he was a betting man, he'd bet the casino that should he push too hard, she'd shove back, just as hard, very likely with a charge of employer harassment.

The thought made him smile.

Maggie narrowed her eyes.

"You're satisfied with the apartment?" The change of subject caught her off guard, as he had figured it would. She blinked again, drawing his

attention to her eyelashes, her long, lush eyelashes. "Everything in working order?"

"Yes, everything works." She nodded. "And
I'm completely satisfied with it." She jerked, as
if having just remembered something important,
and made to turn away. "If you'll tell me the
rental fee, I'll go write out a..."

Mitch stopped her with a sharp hand motion.
He quoted the figure, then quickly added, "But
you can write the check later."

"All right." She raised russet eyebrows, and
once again repeated, "Will there be anything
else?"

"Just one thing," he said. "After you and
Karla have had your coffee, tell her I said she's
to give you a tour of the place, introduce you to
the other employees."

"Yes, si—" she began before catching herself
up short. She drew a breath. "Mitch," she finished, her soft, enticing lips curving into a wry
half smile.

That half smile indicated that she might have
discerned his intentions...at least so far as test-
ing her mettle. As for his ultimate intent, that of
having her soft and warm and eager in his arms,
in his bed, he felt positive she hadn't figured that
one out yet.

But she would, and soon. Maggie was quick and bright, she'd reach that conclusion very soon.

Chuckling to himself, Mitch watched the smooth movement of Maggie's trimly rounded hips and long legs as she crossed to the door. But he was no longer chuckling seconds later, after she had closed the door behind her.

He was aching, in all sorts of uncomfortable places.

Damn thing was, Mitch thought with a sense of both amusement and amazement, he was enjoying the ache, and looking forward to more of the same.

Oh, yeah, he was in big trouble.

Five

He had been baiting her. From their very first meeting, Mitch Grainger had been baiting her.

But... Why?

The question left Maggie in an emotional pickle; she couldn't decide whether to laugh or curse. Never had she dealt with a man so darn confusing. On one hand, Mitch Grainger was arrogant, imperious and irritatingly confident and self-contained. On the other hand...

Come to think of it, what was on the other hand—other than the fact that he was obviously intelligent, attractive as the devil, and exuded sheer masculine sexual magnetism? Maggie mocked herself, uncertain exactly what it was about him that sparked her sense of humor.

The man was absolutely impossible, she thought, smiling at Karla as she left Mitch Grainger's office.

Karla returned Maggie's smile with a frown. "Everything okay?" she asked anxiously. "You were in there an awfully long time."

"Everything's fine," Maggie said, thinking *coffee, coffee, even without caffeine,* as she made a beeline for the coffee machine. "Mr. Grainger told me he had checked out my references." She turned to flash a grin. "Said I checked out in spades."

Karla grinned back. "I just knew you would." The phone rang. "Have your coffee and a pastry," she said, waving at the table before snatching the receiver from the cradle and saying brightly, "This is Karla."

Maggie was munching away happily on an iced cinnamon roll when Karla hung up the phone. It was then she remembered Mitch's instructions.

"Oh, I almost forgot. No, I did forget." Grimacing, she paused to take a sip of the hot brew.

"Mr. Grainger said I was to tell you to give me a tour of the place."

"Oh, good." Karla laughed. "I was just feeling the need to get up and move around a little." The phone rang. She rolled her eyes. "We'll escape as soon as you're finished." Reaching for the phone with one hand, she indicated an identification badge like the one she wore with the other hand, and again snatched up the receiver.

They escaped a few minutes later, the badge bearing Maggie's full name pinned to her lapel.

"From now on, you must wear that at all times in the building," Karla said.

"Right." Maggie nodded, then frowned. "Who'll answer the phone while we're gone?" she asked, casting a worried look at the closed door to Mitch's office.

"If I don't pick up by the third ring, Mitch will," Karla said, leading the way out of the office.

Wonder of wonders, a C.E.O. who'll deign to answer his own phone, Maggie thought, unable to recall any one of her previous employers who would do so. If she were out of the front office, even for a quick trip to the rest room, some lesser executive's secretary was pressed into service.

Why that unimportant tidbit of information about Mitch's apparent willingness to fend for himself should impress her, Maggie hadn't a clue—and yet, it did.

Though it nagged at the back of her mind, Maggie had little chance to examine her odd emotional reaction to Mitch's obvious baiting of her, for Karla began the tour with the first door along the long hallway.

The door led into another set of offices, similar but smaller than Mitch's and Karla's. The front office was manned by a young, nice-looking guy named Roger Knolb. Karla introduced him as the assistant to the assistant manager of the casino, one Rafe Santiago. Rafe was second in command to Mitch.

"You'll have to meet Rafe later," Karla said, waving to Roger as they left the office. "He works the night shift and doesn't come in till around five."

Maggie gave her a puzzled look. "Then why is Roger here now, so early?"

"To handle the regular daytime minutiae," she explained. "Don't forget, most of the rest of the business world keeps nine-to-five hours. Rafe spends most of his time down on the casino floor, as Mitch's eyes, you might say."

They progressed from one room to the next, the rest rooms, the records office, the security office and the money-counting room, where Karla halted one step inside the door, right next to a keen-eyed security guard. Though Karla gave a brief explanation, it really wasn't necessary. The procedure was self-explanatory. Maggie observed the activity in awe, never before in her life having seen so much money in one place.

From the second level, they descended to the main floor. As she had on the office floor, Karla introduced Maggie to every employee they encountered. While every one of them was friendly, they also stirred speculation in Maggie, for every one of them, from the pit boss to the bartender, referred to their employer by his given name. Everywhere they went, it was Mitch this and Mitch that, in tones both casual and respectful.

Odder and odder, Maggie mused.

"Is something bothering you?" Karla asked as they made their way to the far side of the casino floor. "You look puzzled about something."

"It doesn't bother me," Maggie said, quick to clarify her thoughts. "It's just…well, it seems a little unusual to me that all the employees refer to Mr. Grainger by his first name.''

''Oh, that.'' Karla laughed. ''My understanding is that Mitch has always worked on a first-name basis with his employees. He's never played the 'Big Man' role. And so far as I know, at least most of the employees not only respect him, they genuinely like him.''

''But…doesn't that easy, casual manner instill the temptation to take advantage?'' Maggie asked.

Karla smiled. ''With anyone else, it might, probably would. But everyone knows exactly where Mitch stands. He's fair and generous, but he demands absolute loyalty. You see, he has a thing about trust.'' She paused, an odd, fleeting shadow dimming her soft eyes, and she gave a delicate shudder. ''But make no mistake, Mitch can be an unholy terror with anyone who breaks his trust.''

How ironic, Maggie thought. The man had a ''thing'' about trust…whereas she had come to believe that she couldn't or shouldn't trust any man.

''Intimidating, huh?'' Maggie said, wondering what had caused the brief, sad-looking shadow in Karla's eyes, her shudder.

"I'll say." Karla giggled, her sunny disposition restored. "I was so intimidated by him, I was here a long time before I could bring myself to using his first name, and that was only a couple of months ago."

A couple of months ago? Maggie thought in astonishment. Then, that could only mean...

She slid a sidelong glance at Karla's protruding belly. That could only mean she was completely off base in her suspicion that Mitch was the father of Karla's baby.

Which meant that Mitch's concern for Karla was that of a concerned and caring friend as well as her employer, and that Maggie had been condemning him without cause.

The feeling of relief that swept through her was bewildering in its intensity. Why she should feel such relief, Maggie couldn't, or more precisely wouldn't, examine.

Mentally shying away from any deeper meaning in her startled reaction to Karla's laughing remark, Maggie told herself she felt relieved simply because her suspicions were laid to rest and would make working with Mitch a lot less stressful.

From the casino floor, they went to the restaurant where they learned that Mitch had already ordered lunch.

Mitch raised his head at the sound of the outer office door opening, the murmur of feminine voices.

They were back. An anticipatory thrill shot down Mitch's back, tingling the base of his spine. *She* was back.

He grunted in self-disdain when he caught himself straining to distinguish Maggie's voice through his closed office door. At that moment, a tap sounded on the wood panel.

Not wanting to take a chance on being caught with his expectations exposed, Mitch lowered his head and fastened his gaze on the balance sheet in front of him.

"Come in," he said, certain it would be Karla delivering his lunch, hoping it would be Maggie.

The doorknob turned. The door was pushed open. "I have your lunch order from the restaurant upstairs...Mitch."

Maggie.

Mitch hadn't had to hear her voice; he had known it was her the minute she stepped into the room. He had felt her presence, felt as well the same explosive sexual-energy attraction crackling between them he'd felt from the beginning. And she had felt it, too. He could see the awareness of it in her eyes, the infinitesimal quiver of response of her body.

Ruling his expression into a bland mask, Mitch lifted his head. "Thank you, Maggie."

Collecting the pile of printouts and correspondence, he set it to one side, clearing a portion of his desk. Shoving back his chair, he rose, intending to relieve her of the carryout container and drink cup she was holding.

"Don't bother," she said, quickly moving forward to set the containers on the desk. "And you're welcome," she continued, standing straight and alert, as if prepared to bolt the instant he told her she could go. But that flash in her eyes, that minute quiver of her body gave her away.

Oh, yeah, Maggie felt that sizzling attraction as sharply as he did, and she didn't like it. But she would, Mitch promised himself. Eventually, she'd love it, revel in it, every bit as much as he knew he would.

Amused by her wariness, Mitch flicked a hand at the deeply padded chairs in front of his desk. "Have a seat."

Her beautiful green eyes flared with consternation. "But...your lunch will get cold."

Good try, he thought, silently applauding her. "Doesn't matter. It's already cold."

She frowned.

He relented...a little bit. "I ordered a cold sandwich and a cold drink." He inclined his head at the closed cardboard container and tall, lidded waxed paper cup on the tray. "So, please, sit down, Maggie." Though politely phrased, he made it a direct order.

Still she hesitated, uncertainty flickering in her eyes, her expression.

Standing firm, Mitch stared her down—all the way down into the chair placed farthest from him. Conquering an urge to laugh, he reclaimed his seat.

"That's better." He arched a brow. "You and Karla have had lunch?"

"Yes."

Oh, Lord. Her voice sent those fiery fingers girding his hips into overtime. Mitch nodded and cleared his throat. "We can talk while I eat." His hand moved to hover over the closed container. "If you don't mind?"

She answered with a quick shake of her head.

He missed the swirl of her glorious red hair,

now confined in a neat plait at the back of her head. Mitch found himself fighting an impulse to leap up, circle the desk, pull the pins anchoring the strands and spear his fingers into the silky-looking russet mass.

His fingers tingled.

Enjoying the sensation, too much, Mitch swallowed a groan of despair. This was crazy, he thought. Never had he experienced this urgency of desire, this need to be one with a particular woman.

Those green eyes were watching him, shadowed by... What? Mitch asked himself, probing those emerald depths. Fear? Confused awareness? Yes, both, he decided.

Knock it off, Grainger, before you scare her away, he berated himself, wondering what in hell had happened to his normal control.

Flipping open the take-out container, he picked up a triangle of the stacked turkey club sandwich. "Would you like some?" he asked, in what he considered remarkably calm tones, considering his semiarousal and emotional upheaval.

"No, thank you." A near smile kissed her lips; he envied the smile. "As a matter of fact,

I had a turkey club sandwich for lunch, too. It was very good."

Too bad, Mitch mused, biting into the layered sandwich. He would have liked watching her eat.

"You wanted to talk?" Maggie raised her eyebrows.

Not really, what he really wanted was to… Down boy, Mitch cautioned himself, feeling fiery fingers dig hungry claws deep into his groin.

Nodding, he finished chewing and swallowed before answering. "Yes. How was your tour of the premises?"

"Interesting." She gave another half smile, "And a little confusing. And not only the general operation of the business. Karla introduced me to so many of the other employees, all the names ran together. The only ones I remember are the first two, Roger and Rafe, and the last one…Janeen."

Chewing another bite of the sandwich, Mitch nodded again. "It'll take a while," he said, after again swallowing. He washed it down with the cola in the tall cup, trying to think of something else to say to keep her in the office. "You'll learn the ropes soon enough."

"I'm sure," she agreed, then fell silent once more.

"And everything's okay with the apartment?" Damn, Mitch thought, he was reaching, and he knew it. He had asked her that earlier. "Nothing you need?"

"No, everything's fine." Then she frowned. "But about the rental payment...?"

He waved her concern away. "Make the check out to Grainger, Corp. and give it to Karla. She'll take care of it."

"All right." Maggie inched forward on the chair. "Is there anything..."

"No," he interrupted, giving up—for now. "Tell Karla I'll have some tapes to be transcribed later, after I've finished going through the correspondence."

Frustrated, Mitch watched Maggie walk out of the office, unaware that, had she quickly turned back, she'd have seen not only the sexual hunger revealed in his silvered gray eyes, but poignant longing, as well.

Quietly closing Mitch's office door behind her, Maggie was relieved to see Karla busily concentrating on the computer terminal.

Eyes wide with wonder and confusion, Maggie reflected on those emotional and physical electrically charged minutes she had spent in Mitch's company. While she had been aware— too aware—of the force field humming between them before, this time the very air surrounding them seemed to have crackled with the power of the magnetic attraction. It seemed that each time she was near him, the voltage increased.

Nothing anywhere near the conflicting sensations she had experienced during those last few minutes had ever happened to her before. She felt so…so strange, so churned up by myriad feelings of apprehension, incipient panic, simmering excitement and sheer, sizzling sensual tension.

Several times, when Mitch's blatantly passion-fired eyes had pierced hers, as if he were trying to see into the very depths of her mind to her soul, Maggie had literally ceased to breathe, to think.

On the surface, the conversation had all been so casual and mundane. But beneath the surface, Maggie's senses had been bombarded by silent messages.

Without a word, or a move out of line, Mitch had transmitted his desire, his intentions. He wanted her, in the most basic way a man wanted a woman.

It was scary…yet excitingly so.

Needing a few precious seconds to collect herself, Maggie stood silent, inches outside Mitch's door, drawing deep, calming breaths into her oxygen-starved body.

Raising one hand, she stared numbly at the tremor in her fingers. She was trembling inside, too, trembling and…

Again Maggie's breath caught in her throat. She was trembling and aching, tight and hot and moist in the sensitive heart of her femininity.

She wanted him.

The realization battered its way through the barrier of Maggie's self-constructed denial. She had wanted him from the moment she walked into his office that first day and looked into his eyes to feel the power of his masculine attraction to her.

Forewarned by the woman in the restaurant that Mitch Grainger was tough, hard as bedrock, she had been prepared to dislike him on sight. And Maggie had told herself repeatedly over the ensuing days that she had disliked him. She had spent the weekend avoiding the truth that, from that first moment, she had felt irrevocably drawn to him.

How had it happened? Why had it happened? Maggie asked herself, bewildered by her uncharacteristic response to him. She had believed herself sorely lacking in sensuality. She didn't even particularly like sex, had never experienced anything remotely similar to joyous ecstasy while engaged in the act of lovemaking.

Still, her body pulsated with a hollow, aching desire to be one with Mitch Grainger.

What in the world was she going to do? Maggie's first impulse was to bolt, not only from the office, but from the building, straight to the apartment to gather her stuff and hightail it out of Deadwood.

With trembling fingers, Maggie plucked her handbag from the corner of Karla's desk, where she had placed it before entering Mitch's office with his lunch. On shaky legs, she took a step toward the door, and freedom.

"Oh, Maggie," Karla exclaimed on a short laugh, stopping Maggie in her tracks. "I didn't hear you come out of Mitch's office." Her smile gave way to a frown. "You look a little upset. Aren't you feeling well?"

"Yes, I'm fine," Maggie said, raking her

mind for an excuse, any excuse. "I just need to go to the rest room," she improvised.

"Oh..." Karla giggled. "I know the feeling." She flicked a hand at the door. "So...go, you know where it is."

Maggie was through the door like a shot, nearly colliding with Frank, one of the guards, and another man who were right outside. "Oh, excuse me, Frank," she said, feeling foolish as she circled him and the other man. "I'm kind of in a hurry."

Frank chuckled. "Nature calling, huh?"

"Afraid so," she said, her face growing warm with embarrassment. "Too much coffee," she explained, continuing along the hallway to the door marked Women.

Once inside, Maggie slumped back against the door, her pulse racing, her breathing erratic, her body trembling. Staring straight ahead, she was shocked at the sight of her stark reflection in the long mirror above the marble-topped line of sinks.

Startled to her senses by her own pale, distressed image, Maggie drew a deep breath and stiffened her spine. Eyes narrowing, she moved closer to the mirror.

This is nuts, she thought, glaring at her reflection. You're reacting like a twittery teen at the prospect of her first real date.

But, what to do about it? About Mitch?

The impulse to run swept over her again. Exerting every atom of willpower she possessed, Maggie quashed the thought out of existence.

Damned if she would run, she lectured herself. She had been running for months, only to learn, finally, that she couldn't run from herself. Her anger, her uncertainties were always with her.

Well, she had decided to stop running, hadn't she? Maggie reminded herself. She had settled into the apartment, determined to stand firm, to face and deal with whatever life threw at her.

But...Mitch Grainger? Could she deal with him? Or, more important, her wildly sensual reaction to him?

Worrying the questions, Maggie gnawed at her lip, only then noticing she had eaten off her lipstick along with her lunch. She could use some color in her cheeks, as well.

Pull it together, she advised herself, turning on the cold water tap to bathe the still-racing pulse in her wrists. Turning off the tap, she dried her hands with a paper towel, then dabbed at the moist line of perspiration on her brow and at the back of her neck.

Cooler, calmer, feeling more composed, Maggie removed the small makeup pouch from her handbag and set to repairing her appearance.

Minutes later, Maggie critically studied her renewed reflection. She allowed herself a faint smile of satisfaction for the effort at camouflage. The shine on her forehead, nose and chin had been concealed by a few pats of translucent pressed-powder foundation. Her cheeks glowed with healthy-looking, if artificial, color, the muted red applied to her full lips was outlined with a darker hue.

Warpaint on, Maggie squared her shoulders. She would not run. She was done with running. She would stay and face not only Mitch Grainger, but her own overwhelming attraction to him.

Curving her lips into a pleasant smile, Maggie turned and marched back to the office.

Six

Moving back into the office quietly so as not to disturb Karla, Maggie slipped into a chair in front of the desk. Taking her checkbook from her bag, she wrote out the rental payment on the apartment. She was tearing the check from the book when Karla turned away from the screen to smile at her.

"Oh, I'm glad you're back," she said, pushing her chair back and easing out of it. "Now I have to go...urgently." She grinned. "You can man the phone."

"Mitch told me to give the rent payment to you," Maggie said, holding up the check.

Already at the door, Karla said, "Lay it on the desk, I'll take care of it when I get back."

Man the phones. Great, what'll I do if the darn thing rings? What'll I say? Sorry, but I'm new and don't know diddly about the business yet? Now, that would make a sterling impression, Maggie thought, grimacing as she moved around the desk and settled into Karla's chair. She had just decided that her best bet was to pray the phone didn't ring, when the darn thing did.

Maggie warily eyed the phone through the second ring, then recalling Karla saying that if it wasn't answered by the third ring Mitch would pick it up, she grabbed the receiver.

"This is Maggie," she said, in the same manner as Karla always answered.

"Maggie? What happened to Karla?" the caller, a woman, asked in an ultracool, rather haughty tone.

An old hand at dealing with all types of calls, from all types of people, Maggie was less than impressed, but scrupulously professional. "Karla is out of the office at the moment," she responded pleasantly. "May I help you?"

"Yes," Ms. Haughty snapped back. "You

may put me through to Mitch.'' Not a request; an order.

As if, Maggie thought, raising her eyebrows. ''I'll see if Mr. Grainger can take your call,'' she said, ever so sweetly. ''Whom shall I say is calling?''

''Natalie Crane.'' The woman's superior tones suggested her name alone opened all doors.

''Please hold.'' Witch, Maggie added to herself, immediately hitting the hold button. She waited with calm deliberation for a full thirty seconds before buzzing Mitch.

''Yes, Karla?''

The sound of his voice reactivated the quiver inside Maggie. For an instant, her mind went blank, her throat went dry. Idiot, she chastised herself, clearing her throat.

''Karla?''

''It's Maggie,'' she quickly responded. ''Karla's out of the office.''

He chuckled. ''Ladies' room, huh?''

''Yes.'' She had to smile.

''What can I do for you, Maggie?''

The ideas that sprang to her mind didn't bear thinking about. Shocked at herself, Maggie rushed into speech. "There's a call for you on line two...a Ms. Natalie Crane."

A pause, then he said, "Get rid of her," in a hard-sounding near growl, before disconnecting.

Oh, my, Maggie thought, so much for opening all doors. Happy to oblige, she released the hold button. "I'm sorry, Ms. Crane, but Mr. Grainger is in conference and can't take your call right now. May I take a message?"

"Yes," Ms. Haughty snapped. "Tell him I expect him to return my call as soon as he is out of conference."

Maggie winced as the receiver was slammed down at the other end of the line. "Well, goodbye to you, too," she murmured, smiling with satisfaction.

"Who was that?"

Not having heard the office door open, Maggie started at the sound of Karla's voice. "Oh, Karla," she said, her smile widening. "Feel better?"

"Umm," Karla nodded, and grinned. "At least for another hour or so. Who were you talking to?"

"An unpleasant woman named Natalie Crane," Maggie drawled. "She demanded to speak to Mitch."

Karla made a face. "The Popsicle Princess."

"Popsicle Princess?" Maggie laughed. "Why do you call her that?"

Karla laughed with her. "Because she's cold as ice, and has very little substance." Her laughter gave way to a frown. "What did Mitch say?"

"He refused to talk to her." She lowered her voice. "In fact, he told me to get rid of her."

"I'm not surprised," Karla confided. "He can be utterly unrelenting at times."

A terror and unrelenting, Maggie mused, suppressing a shudder. Wonderful. The strange thing was, the shudder was made up of equal parts of trepidation and…and…surely not a sense of fascination and excitement? Of course not, she assured herself, while at the same time speculation whispered through her mind about whether some of those unrelenting times might occur when he was in bed, with a woman. More to the point, was Natalie Crane one such woman?

Although Maggie tried to contain her curiosity, she had to ask, "And he's unrelenting with this particular woman?"

"Yes." Karla sighed. "She's called here several times, but he absolutely refuses to speak to her."

Unrelenting indeed, Maggie mused, her curiosity unanswered by Karla's response. But, telling herself it was really none of her business, Maggie refrained from questioning Karla further on the subject.

"Is his visitor still in there?"

Jarred from her musings by the question, Maggie blinked. "Visitor?" she repeated, getting up and moving around the desk so Karla could sit down. "He has a visitor?"

"Yes." Karla nodded, settling into the chair. "Frank brought him in right after you went out." She frowned. "Didn't you see them?"

"Oh, yes," Maggie said, her smile wry. "I nearly ran smack into Frank. But I was in such a rush, I didn't notice the man with him."

"You're kidding," Karla exclaimed. "Gosh, I'd have taken notice of him in a crowded room."

Maggie laughed. "Good-looking, huh?"

"I'll say." Karla heaved a dramatic, exaggerated sigh and placed a hand on her chest. "Be still, my heart."

"Wow," Maggie said, playing along with the fun. "I can't wait to see…" She broke off when the sound of men's voices preceded the opening of Mitch's door.

The man who emerged from the office ahead of Mitch was good-looking, tall and lean, but the sight of him didn't set Maggie's heart to fluttering. That feat was accomplished by Mitch, coming to a halt in the doorway, his silvered eyes piercing hers before shifting to Karla.

Mitch introduced the man as Ben Daniels, an old friend of the Grainger family. As greetings and handshakes were exchanged, Maggie couldn't help but notice the flare of keen awareness in Ben's eyes each time he looked at Karla.

Interesting, Maggie thought. She wondered if Ben's attention was personal in nature or mere curiosity at Karla's obvious pregnancy and equally obvious lack of a wedding ring.

"Karla, Ben will be in town a couple of weeks on vacation," Mitch said. "I told him you had some brochures for the local attractions you could give him."

"Oh, sure, have a seat," she invited, tearing her gaze from the man to reach for the bottom desk drawer.

"Thank you, ma'am," Ben said, lowering his long frame into one of the chairs in front of her desk.

"I'm going to get back to work, Ben," Mitch said. "Stop by anytime, and good luck at the tables." A slow grin curled his lips, and Maggie's toes. "Except mine, of course." With a casual wave of his hand, he turned away.

Beginning to feel like the third wheel on a bicycle, Maggie moved to go to the small table she had used the previous week to fill out the job application.

"Oh, Maggie, is there any coffee left?" Mitch asked, turning back into the doorway.

"Yes." Maggie glanced at the pot, noting that it had been sitting, with the warmer plate on, since that morning. "But it must be bitter by now," she added. "Would you like me to make a fresh pot?"

"Yes...if you don't mind?" His tone and one arched brow had a sardonic cast.

"Not at all," Maggie said.

"Thank you." He again turned from the door.

"You're welcome." Crossing to the coffee-maker, Maggie could hear Karla explaining to Ben Daniels the self-explanatory information contained in several different brochures.

The two were still discussing the pros and cons of the various sights of interest when, a few minutes later, Maggie carried a fresh cup of coffee into Mitch's office.

"That smells good, thank you," Mitch said as

she set the cup close to hand on his desk. Inner amusement gave his gray eyes a teasing glimmer. "But I miss the caffeine kick."

Maggie laughed aloud. "I know what you mean. I fortified myself with two cups of the real thing at lunch."

"Lucky you. I guess that's what I should have done." He took a careful sip. "But this'll do."

Taking that as a dismissal, Maggie nodded and turned to leave. "If you want a refill just..." she began, breaking off when she suddenly remembered the earlier call. "Oh, yes," she said, turning back to face him. "Ms. Crane left a message requesting you return her call."

In the process of taking another sip of coffee, Mitch muttered something that sounded suspiciously like a suggestion as to what Ms. Crane could do to herself.

"I beg your pardon?" Maggie said, positive she had not heard him correctly.

"Never mind." The glimmer in Mitch's eyes took on a devilish glint. "I really don't think you'd want to hear the remark repeated. I wouldn't want to shock your delicate sensibilities."

So, she hadn't misheard him, Maggie thought,

giving him a droll look, and a dry-voiced response. "I suspect I've heard worse."

"Hmm," he murmured, around the rim of the cup he'd raised to his mouth. He swallowed deeply and held the cup out. "Did you mention something about a refill?"

"Yes." Stepping forward, she reached for the cup. The tips of her fingers brushed the backs of his. The brief touch of his skin against hers caused a prickling sensation. It took all Maggie's will to keep from pulling her hand back, out of harm's way. "I'll...er...be back in a minute," she said, grasping the cup and hurrying from the room.

Maybe it was her imagination, but Maggie could have sworn she heard the rich sound of his muffled laughter.

To her surprise, Karla and Ben were still deep in conversation. Moving quietly, Maggie crossed to the coffeemaker and refilled Mitch's cup. To her amusement, neither Karla nor Ben appeared to take notice of her as she returned to Mitch's office.

Once again, Maggie walked to his desk and set the cup close to hand, her spine tingling in response to the intentness of his steady gaze monitoring her every step.

Damn, how was it that this man could make her feel all nervy and quivery just by looking at her? Maggie wondered, steeling herself to meet and hold his consuming stare.

"Thank you."

The low, sexy sound of his voice shot adrenaline into her system. "You're welcome," she replied, despairing her own breathy, whispery tones. "Will there be anything else?"

"Yes." He smiled, slowly, sensuously, sending a silent message that raised the short hairs at her nape. Picking up a sheaf of papers, he held them out to her. "This batch of correspondence requires only a general form-letter response. Karla will show you how it's done."

Wonder of wonders, a boss who'll answer the phone and sift through the correspondence, Maggie thought, careful not to touch him as she took the papers.

Noting her reluctance to so much as brush his fingers with her own, Mitch's eyes danced with deviltry.

Torn between annoyance and amusement, Maggie beat a hasty retreat. This time she was certain she heard his soft laughter following in her wake.

Shivering with sensitive awareness, of herself

as a woman, of Mitch as a man in pursuit, Maggie breathed a sigh of relief as she shut his door behind her.

Fortunately, Karla didn't hear or even see her. Alone now in the office, the pregnant woman sat still as a stone, staring into space, a bemused expression on her pretty face.

Maggie moved to the side of the desk. "Karla?"

"Oh, Maggie." Karla blinked and blushed.

"You look strange," Maggie said with concern. "Are you feeling all right?"

"Yes..." she said, her cheeks glowing with color. "Yes, I'm fine. Really." She laughed. "Ben's invited the two of us to dinner. Please say you'll go."

"Well, of course I'll go, but..."

"I think he's terrific," Karla quickly added. She glanced down at her protruding belly and sighed, her color fading. "And I believe he's interested in you."

Maggie couldn't help smiling at the very idea. It had been obvious to her that Ben had taken an immediate shine to Karla. "I seriously doubt that," she said. "He barely looked at me. Perhaps he would just like some feminine company,'' she suggested. ''Since he's here on his own.''

''Maybe you're right,'' Karla agreed, brightening. ''He's so nice, soft-spoken and gentle.''

''He's a hellion,'' Mitch said with hard-voiced conviction.

Neither woman had heard him open his door. Maggie jumped. Karla squealed in shocked surprise.

''Sorry if I startled you,'' he apologized, while sounding not a bit sorry.

''That was a terrible thing to say about Ben,'' Karla reproached him, her eyes shadowed with disappointment. ''I thought you said he was a family friend.''

''He is, but that doesn't change the fact that he was always a hellion and a devil with the ladies,'' Mitch retorted. ''Though I will admit that Justin claims Ben has changed his ways the past few years.''

''Justin?'' Maggie asked, frowning at the unfamiliar name, although it was really none of her business.

''Justin Grainger.'' Karla supplied the answer. ''Mitch's brother. He runs the family horse ranch in Montana.''

''Ben works for Justin,'' Mitch added.

"Okay, I've got the picture," Maggie said, puzzled by the whole conversation, though she did have some suspicions. "But why did you want us to know about Ben's reputation?"

Mitch favored her with a hard stare. "I overheard Karla say he had invited the two of you to dinner."

Bingo. Maggie arched a brow. "So?"

His eyes narrowed. "I just thought you should know that he has a reputation so far as women are concerned."

"It's only for dinner, Mitch," Karla protested, her dejected tone a clear indication to Maggie that if he said she shouldn't go, she wouldn't.

Like hell, Maggie thought. There was no way she was going to allow Mitch to dictate to either her or Karla as to how and with whom they spent their free time.

"And we're going," Maggie stated, her voice firm with stark challenge.

Hope flared to life in Karla's eyes, cementing Maggie's determination. It was all so silly, really, she thought, glaring at Mitch. What earthly harm could there be in having dinner with the man?

To Mitch's credit, he gave in gracefully. "Of

course, I can't stop you from going. What you two do on your own time is your business."

"That's right, it is." Maggie continued to hold his steady stare, which hadn't softened a whit.

"Just be careful," he advised, turning to go back to his office.

"I always am. And I'll take care of Karla, too." Maggie's wry assurance stopped him in the doorway.

"Hey," Karla yelped. "I can take care of myself."

"Right," he drawled, his gaze dropping to her distended belly.

Karla blushed.

Maggie bristled. "We all make mistakes," she snapped in Karla's defense, while reflecting on her own mistake in trusting Todd, convincing herself she'd been in love with him. "I'd wager even you have made your share."

"A few," he admitted, closing the subject by stepping into his office and shutting the door.

"Wow," Karla said in admiration. "I've never heard anyone talk back to him like that before."

"Oh, for heaven's sake," Maggie said, rolling her eyes. "He's a man, not a god."

"He's the boss," Karla reminded her.

"Not of my free time, or yours," Maggie retorted. "And not over whomever we choose to spend that time with. However, we're on his time now, so I guess we'd better get to work."

Dammit, he really screwed that one up, Mitch thought, cursing his heavy-handedness. He should have known Maggie would defy him, even on her very first day in the office. Hell, hadn't she been silently challenging his authority since the first day she walked into the office? And hadn't her open defiance been one of her attractions?

Despite his frustration, Mitch had to chuckle. But his chuckle dissolved into a low growl at the very real possibility that Ben, like Mitch himself, had instantly developed an appreciation for Maggie's many attractions. Why else would he have so quickly invited the women to have dinner with him?

Mitch had already dismissed the notion that Karla might be the reason for Ben's interest. Not because Karla was unattractive—she was a lovely young woman, inside and out. But, as she also was very pregnant, it stretched credulity to conclude that Ben's gaze had skipped over Maggie to land on Karla.

No, Mitch was convinced Ben had designs on Maggie, and the idea of them, possibly alone together in Maggie's apartment after Karla had retired for the night, bugged the hell out of him.

His imagination ran wild, and rather erotic, throughout that night...and the other two nights Ben escorted the two women during that week. Mitch knew about the successive dates, because the women talked freely about them. And, for all he knew, the three of them might well have gone traipsing off together over the weekend, as well.

By the next Monday, Mitch was not in the best of moods or frame of mind. Seething inside at having his own plans for Maggie usurped by Ben's appearance on the scene, he reacted by presenting a cool, remote demeanor in the office.

Looking bewildered and apprehensive, Karla fairly tiptoed around him.

Maggie, conversely, went about the business of learning her duties with commendable competence and a calm reserve belied by the glitter of defiance in her green eyes.

In regard to her competence, Mitch had expected no less, after receiving that rave review from her former employer. Yet even so, he was impressed by her efficiency, her quick grasp of the day-to-day running of the business.

As to the blatant defiance in Maggie's eyes, her thinly veiled look of challenge each time their gazes met and locked, that both thrilled and annoyed him.

It was a maddening situation for Mitch, as never before in his life had a woman so irritated him, while at the same time arousing within him such deep instincts of physical hunger and possessiveness.

Something had to crack, and soon, Mitch decided. He only hoped that something wouldn't be him.

What on earth was the matter with the irascible man?

Maggie asked herself that same question about Mitch Grainger at least a dozen times during those first two weeks of her employment with him.

She was beginning to wonder if Mitch could possess multiple personalities. It was the only thing she could think of to explain his sudden, inexplicable switches.

With each successive day, Mitch was proving

more difficult for Maggie to characterize. But he was definitely more complex than she had first believed. Bedrock-hard and tough? Yes, that he was. Somewhat arrogant and intimidating? That, too. A man definitely in control? In spades.

On the other hand Mitch was not above preparing the morning coffee before she and Karla had arrived for work. He'd also answer the phone and sort through the mail whenever they were out of the office on some errand.

In addition, it quickly became obvious to Maggie that there was a regularity to Mitch's leaving his office for an hour or two every other day or so. The third time he did so, she voiced her curiosity about his purpose.

"Oh, he's making the rounds of the place, the other offices, the casino floor, even the bar and restaurant…keeping contact with the employees," Karla told her. "Not checking *up* on them," she quickly clarified. "But checking *in* with them, keeping the lines of communication open."

On a first-name basis, Maggie had thought, recalling her surprise on hearing everyone refer to Mitch that way. A two-way street of the trust and loyalty thing. Commendable…and also very smart.

Almost against her will, Maggie felt a growing respect for the man, both as an employer and a male.

Yet, at the same time her respect for him was growing, he continued to unsettle her. And the most baffling thing of all for Maggie was the complete change in his approach to her, from his initial droll, teasing attitude, to one of withdrawn, near icy remoteness.

Yet for all his surface coldness and hard-edged tones, there was still a smoldering passion blazing from his silver-sheened eyes every time he captured her gaze.

It was unnerving, because it excited Maggie so very much. It stirred her up inside, made her feel feverish and chilly at the same time.

Maggie found the job as personal assistant to the C.E.O. of a gambling casino an interesting departure from her previous employment. But working for the icy-voiced, hot-eyed Mitch, eight hours a day, five days a week, was sheer torment with a generous dash of delicious danger. Each time she entered his office she was never quite certain of what he might say or—even more unsettling and secretly more exciting—what he might do.

For Maggie, each morning she walked into the

office was like stepping onto a tightrope. And it amazed her that Karla seemed serenely unaware of the energy simmering in the atmosphere.

But then Karla, while scrupulous in teaching Maggie every nuance of the job, was floating in a rosy cloud of infatuation with Ben Daniels.

That Ben was equally infatuated with Karla was obvious. In fact, by their second evening out with him, Karla had accepted Maggie's first impression that Ben's interest had always been for Karla.

And yet when, after their third dinner date with Ben, Maggie had suggested begging off on future evenings out so that Karla and Ben could have some time alone together, Karla had objected. Her past experiences with the still-undisclosed father of her child continued to make her wary of Ben's ultimate intentions.

While she fully understood Karla's apprehensions, Maggie's impression of Ben was that of a down-to-earth, honest and dependable man. And her initial impression of him went up a notch when he had gently suggested to Karla, as Maggie herself had numerous times, that she tell her parents about her condition.

But then, impressions could be deceiving, she reminded herself. Hadn't she trusted Todd?

Her second week in the office was pure torture for Maggie, and she began to rue her own expertise. Wanting to save Karla as much of the legwork as possible—since her expanding condition was obviously making it noticeably more difficult to get in and out of her chair—Maggie took on the responsibility of responding every time Mitch called for one of them to come into his office.

Merely crossing the threshold into his office became an ongoing torment, for Maggie was struck, weakened, by the electrically charged magnetic waves of physical attraction emanating between them. The sensuous sensations aroused within her were breathtaking, exciting, demoralizing.

On each occasion, Maggie exited Mitch's office feeling shaken, hungry, yearning for...

It didn't bear thinking about.

By Friday, Maggie was seriously considering flinging herself into Mitch's arms, offering herself up to the heated passion in his eyes, if only to end the sensual agony.

But, of course, Maggie didn't do any such thing. Quitting time Friday did finally arrive and, along with it, Ben Daniels. He was taking her and Karla out one last time as he was leaving to return to Montana early the next morning.

Although Ben had made a solemn promise to Karla to return to Deadwood in December and to be with her for the birth of her baby, Karla's spirits were low at the prospect of Ben's imminent departure.

Maggie was laughing and chattering away with Ben, who was equally animated, in hopes of lightening Karla's dejected mood, when Mitch's office door suddenly opened.

"Hi, Ben," Mitch greeted the other man, rather coolly, in Maggie's opinion. "Heading out tomorrow?"

"Yeah." Ben sighed, but worked up a smile. "So tonight Karla, Maggie and I are going to live it up."

"I'm sorry, but I'm afraid I have to interfere with your plans." Avoiding Maggie's surprised look, he turned to Karla. "A fax just came in that necessitates an immediate and lengthy response. I need you to stay late, Karla."

"We'll wait," Ben offered at once. "Won't we, Maggie?"

"No," Maggie was quick to assert, noting the gleam of disappointed tears in Karla's eyes. "You two go on ahead. I'll stay," she volunteered, wondering at the flash of bewilderment in Mitch's eyes. "That is, if it's all right with you?"

"Yes, of course," Mitch said, his voice sounding odd, almost stunned.

"Oh, but..." Karla began, in token protest.

"No, buts," Maggie cut in. "I know where you're going. Maybe I can catch up with you later."

"Well...if you insist," Karla said uncertainly, looking at Ben for guidance.

"Are you sure, Maggie?" Ben asked. "We really don't mind waiting."

"Go, go," Maggie said, exasperated by their display of reluctance, when she knew they wanted to be alone together, especially this last night of Ben's vacation.

"See you, Ben," Mitch said, shooting a puzzled glance between Maggie and Karla before turning back into his office.

"Yeah, see you," Ben called after him. "Ready, Karla?" he asked, taking her arm.

Karla looked undecided.

"Will you go already?" Maggie said, heaving a noisy sigh. "You're wasting time. I'll never get done here at this rate."

"Well..." Karla hedged.

"Go," Maggie ordered.

Grinning, Ben gave Maggie a thumbs-up as he hustled Karla out the door.

Grinning back, Maggie responded with a happy nod. But her grin faded with the shutting of the door behind them.

The question of whether she could handle the job before her should have been uppermost in her mind. It wasn't. No, what took command of her thinking was whether she could handle her employer. But it wasn't a fear that she couldn't handle him that gave Maggie pause, but the very real possibility that she wouldn't want to.

Taking a deep breath, and drawing her composure around her like a shield, Maggie followed Mitch into his office.

He was standing in front of his desk, his expression contemplative. A slow smile tugged at his lips as Maggie crossed to him.

"Alone at last."

Seven

Alone at last?

Momentarily stunned by Mitch's murmured remark, Maggie stared at him with wary suspicion.

Had his claim about the urgent need to respond to a late-arriving fax been just a ploy to get her alone?

Excitement flared to life inside her. Yet even as it came into her mind, Maggie rejected the question. Mitch had had no idea that she would offer to remain, had in fact asked Karla to stay.

So, then, why had he said...

"Don't freak, Maggie," he drawled, making a half turn to pick up the fax on his desk. "Trust me, I have no intentions of bushwhacking you."

"I wasn't about to 'freak'," Maggie informed him, arching a brow in disdain. "And I don't *trust* any man," she said with hard emphasis.

He went stone still for a moment, as if in personal affront, then a wry smile flickered over his lips and he raised one dark eyebrow. "Not even Ben Daniels?"

"Ben is very nice, charming and good company," Maggie said, wondering what Ben had to do with anything. "But, he is still a man."

"I see," he murmured. "You've been bushwhacked before, and the wounds inflicted are still raw."

Well, that was a fairly accurate description, Maggie reflected. She had felt bushwhacked when she'd read that damned note Todd had left for her, and the emotional wounds were still raw, despite her acceptance of never really having been in love with him in the first place. But, naturally, she wasn't about to admit as much to Mitch.

"Is disclosure about my personal life, past and present, part of my job description?" she countered, mirroring his single raised eyebrow.

"No, of course not," he conceded. "What you do on your own time is entirely your own business." He managed a small but genuine smile. "So long as it's legal."

"Glad to hear it," Maggie drawled. "That being the case," she continued, pointedly glancing at the fax he was holding, "I suggest we get to the business at hand."

Mitch actually chuckled. "You don't rattle easily, do you?" he said, gliding a molten, silvery look over her.

"I don't rattle at all," she retorted, knowing it was a bare-faced lie, as the heat, the blatantly hungry glitter in his eyes, had her hot and bothered and rattled something fierce.

"All right." Giving a brisk nod, he raised the fax. "This came in a short time ago. It's from Adam. He needs some information from us…a lot of information, and he needs it by Monday morning."

Naturally, by the end of her second week on the job, Maggie knew that Adam Grainger was the president of the Grainger Corporation, the head honcho of its diverse operations. Taking the fax sheet Mitch held out to her, she carefully read the terse, concise instructions, concluded that Mitch was right, his brother did want a lot of information.

Rereading the fax, Maggie raised her eyebrows.

"Adam recently picked up some dependable murmurings about the financial difficulties of a riverboat casino," Mitch said, answering her silent question. He named the parent group of a chain of casinos.

Unfamiliar with any but the most publicized of the casino groups and owners, the name meant nothing to Maggie, and she admitted as much.

"Doesn't matter," Mitch said. "What does matter is that Adam got word that the group was planning to file bankruptcy. He contacted the president of the group this morning, suggesting the possibility of a full takeover by Grainger Corp." He smiled. "They must be eager to unload, because a meeting was set up for Monday morning. Naturally, Adam intends to be well armed with comparison data, thus this rushed request."

Naturally, Maggie thought. She was inordinately pleased by the confidence implied by Mitch's comprehensive explanation, when he could have simply ordered her to retrieve the information without giving her a reason.

"Then, I guess I'd better get to work," she said.

As expected, gathering and retrieving the requested data proved to be a lengthy process. Immersed in the work, Maggie was only peripherally aware of Mitch moving around in his office. The sound of his voice as he spoke on the phone wafted to her through the open doorway.

Sometime later, she saw him leave his office and exit through the door to the hallway, vaguely thinking he was off to make one of his periodic swings through the casino floor.

"Time for a break, Maggie."

Not having heard him reenter the office, she started at the sound of his voice, clueless as to how long he'd been gone. "I've just finished gathering the info. I was ready to start faxing it." Turning away from the computer screen, she saw he was carrying a tray, laden with covered dishes.

"I've brought us some dinner." He held the tray aloft. "Leave that for later and come eat."

Grateful for the opportunity to stretch her stiff

neck, back and legs, Maggie stood. She followed him into his office, to the small round table between the two narrow windows that looked out onto Main Street.

Mitch set the large tray on the table, then pulled out one of the deeply padded leather captain's chairs for her. "You relax," he ordered gently. "I'll play server."

Settling into the comfortable chair, Maggie gave him an impish smile. "Will you expect a tip?"

"Certainly." Smiling back at her, he proceeded to transfer the covered dishes, utensils, two cups and a tall thermos of coffee from the tray to the table.

"Okay, don't bet on a draw for an inside straight," she quipped, deadpan, expecting him to laugh.

Setting the tray aside, Mitch seated himself opposite her before replying, his tone serious. "You'll have to do better than that...because I never gamble on games of chance."

Surprised by his remark, Maggie blurted out the first thought that sprang to mind. "You run a casino and you never gamble?"

"That's right." He smiled with wry humor. "Life itself is enough of a gamble for me."

"Incredible," she murmured, lifting the cover off the plate he'd set before her. She inhaled the mouth-watering aromas of filet of sole in lemon butter, chunks of roasted potatoes and green beans with slivered almonds. "Thank you for this," she said appreciatively. "It looks and smells wonderful."

"You're welcome," Mitch replied, standing to pick up the thermos and circle the table to pour her coffee. "And here's the best part." He grinned. "It's caffeinated."

"Pure decadence," she said, laughing.

His grin was infectious. *He* was infectious. As he bent over to pour the steaming brew into her cup, Maggie caught the heady fragrance of his spicy cologne, and the even more heady scent of musky male.

Decadence, indeed. He was more tempting than the beautifully prepared food on her plate. In that instant, Maggie was uncomfortably aware of an earthy hunger more powerful than her body's need for mere food and drink.

"I had considered a crisp white wine to go with the fish," Mitch was saying, returning to the chair opposite her. "But figured you'd prefer the coffee."

"You figured correctly," Maggie said, thinking the look of him, the scent of him, the nearness of him was enough to fog her senses.

"I wanted you clearheaded."

Maggie nearly choked on the bite of fish in her mouth. Could he mean...? No. Surely not, she told herself. He must have been referring to the fax still to be sent, not a desire for something intimate between them.

"Of course," she agreed, after managing to swallow the mangled bite of sole. "Understandable."

She raised her cup to her lips.

He smiled...a slow, sexy smile.

Maggie scalded her tongue on the hot coffee.

As the meal progressed, Maggie grew steadily more nervous and churned up inside. It didn't help matters that she couldn't seem to stop glancing at his mouth every time he took a forkful of food or a sip from his cup. He had a beautiful male mouth, the upper lip thin, the lower slightly fuller, more sensuous. She felt she could almost taste it along with her food and drink.

It was pure heaven.

It was sheer hell.

It was finally over.

Barely tasting the food she'd consumed, Maggie was amazed that she had cleaned her plate of every morsel. Even so, she still felt hungry, empty and needy.

Get back to work, to reality, Maggie scolded herself. Setting her napkin beside her plate, she pushed back her chair, stood and began clearing the table.

"Leave it," Mitch ordered. Rising, he circled the table to pluck the plate from her suddenly trembling fingers.

"But…" Maggie began, her voice trailing away as she looked up, stopped breathing and got lost inside his silvery eyes.

"I'm going to kiss you, Maggie."

It was a fair-enough warning, Maggie allowed. He didn't move or lower his head, giving her a moment to protest or retreat if she chose to do so. She didn't. Instead, she raised her head to give him her response, and better access to her mouth.

"Yes, please."

Something flickered in his eyes. Surprise? Delight? Maggie didn't know, nor did she care, for he slowly lowered his head to claim her mouth with his own.

Shooting stars. Exploding rockets. And yes, the earth moving under her feet. Maggie felt cer-

tain she experienced every one of those phenom-
ena, plus sensations too numerous to count.

She wanted, she needed…more.

So, obviously, did Mitch. His arms coiled
around her, drawing her into intimate contact
with his hardening body. His mouth devoured
hers. His tongue thrust deep to scour the sweetness of her mouth.

Curling her arms around his taut neck, Maggie
vaguely heard a low groan of need, but wasn't
sure if it came from his throat or her own. She
could taste the coffee he had drunk, and the dis-
tinct, mind-clouding flavor of pure Mitch. Wanting more and more of his taste she clung to his
mouth, to him. She couldn't breathe. She didn't
care. At that moment, she'd have happily died
in the all-consuming fire of his kiss.

But, apparently, Mitch had a different kind of
death in mind for both of them. Pulling his head
back, he stared at her, his eyes molten silver with
passion. Loosening his hold, he moved away,
toward a door set into the wall a few feet behind
them.

Maggie blinked in confusion. Where was he
going? she wondered. Of course, she had noticed
the door before, and had assumed it opened into

a storage area, or perhaps even Mitch's private bathroom.

"Come with me, Maggie," he said, extending one hand to her, while grasping the doorknob with the other. "Please."

He wanted her to go with him into a closet…or a bathroom? But, even as the question flashed through her mind, Maggie took a step forward and slid her hand into his.

The door opened to reveal an enclosed staircase, and it was then Maggie recalled Karla saying that Mitch had an apartment on the third level.

Butterflies were doing bumps and grinds in her stomach, but she allowed Mitch to lead her up the carpeted stairs.

The staircase opened onto a spacious landing. A large living area was located to the left and a hallway ran straight to the back of the building.

Maggie barely had time to see the living area, getting a mere glimpse of large, overstuffed furniture in midnight blue and white. With a tug on her hand, Mitch drew her to an open door along the hallway.

Legs trembling, she preceded him into his bedroom, flinching when he swung the door shut behind them.

Alone at last.

The echo of his words of a few hours ago rang inside her head. Only here and now, they were really alone...together...in his bedroom. The king-size bed loomed enormous in Maggie's sight, blurring her vision to any other furniture, the overall color scheme.

An instant of panic gripped Maggie at the touch of his hand on her shoulder. She froze for long seconds, motionless with indecision.

What did she think she was doing? a scared inner voice demanded.

Oh, don't be such a wuss, go for it, a braver voice insisted.

She fought the urge to bolt, with the stronger urge to stay. Would being with Mitch, in the most intimate of ways, be any different? She gulped a strangled breath and turned to face him.

"You can change your mind, Maggie," he said, his features taut with self-imposed control.

Her gaze lowered to his mouth, those lips that had turned her gray matter to soggy granules. Excitement leaped like a flame inside her, spreading like wildfire throughout her entire being. She wanted that mouth, those lips on hers, doing crazy, erotic things to her.

"Don't look at me like that." His voice was soft, harsh.

"Like what?" Her voice was barely there.

"Like you want to devour me."

"I do." In that instant her decision was made. "But only if you promise to devour me in return."

Exhaling the breath she hadn't realized he was holding, Mitch groaned and pulled her into his arms. "That's a promise I'll be happy to fulfill," he murmured, lowering his head to take her mouth.

The devouring process had begun.

Heat consuming her, Maggie was only vaguely aware of Mitch moving her toward the bed, of his fingers plucking the pins from her hair, of his hands divesting her of her clothes, of her own hands tugging at his attire. But within minutes, they stood next to the bed, facing each other, the trappings of civilization littering the floor around them.

"Beautiful," he said, slowly gliding his hot-eyed gaze over her body.

"Yes, you are," she whispered, returning the compliment with an appreciative examination of his tall and fit muscular body, the awesome length of his manhood.

He chuckled. "Men aren't beautiful," he scoffed, raising his hands to cradle her breasts with a near reverent touch. "They're beautiful."

"They're too small." She sighed, quivering as his fingers stroked the tingling, tightening tips. "They barely fill out a B-cup bra."

"They fill my palms." He closed his hands around her breasts, claiming them for his own. "Perfect."

Obeying the boldest impulse she had ever had, Maggie slid her hand down his torso and curled her fingers around him. "So are you."

Mitch drew in a sharp breath, thrust his hips forward, closed his eyes and groaned. "I think we'd better lie down...before I fall down."

"Yes," Maggie agreed in a wavery voice, feeling rather light-headed herself.

Mitch paused long enough to toss the comforter and top sheet to the foot of the bed. Settling her in the center of the mattress, he sought, captured her mouth as he stretched out beside her.

Maggie's mind was on the verge of taking a leave of absence when a thought popped in out of nowhere. Tearing her lips from his, she cried, "Mitch, the fax!"

"Screw the fax," he growled, stabbing the

corner of her mouth with the tip of his tongue. "On second thought, I'd much rather scr..." He shook his head. "No, not with you. With you, I want to make love."

Thrilled, shivering in anticipation, Maggie caught his head with her hands, speared her fingers into his luxurious dark hair. "Does making love include devouring?"

He laughed, a rich, free-sounding roar. "Of course."

"Then, get on with it," she commanded, laughing with him as she drew his mouth to hers.

Eight

Mitch propped himself up on his arm and looked over at Maggie, who was curled up beside him, sound asleep. His mind still on stun, Mitch studied her face and her form in awed astonishment.

Maggie had not been a virgin. Mitch had not expected her to be untouched, not in her late twenties. But, to his complete surprise, he had quickly realized that she was woefully untutored, a near innocent to sensual play. To his delight, she had proved not only willing but eager to learn and had shyly, yet trustingly following his lead.

For Mitch, Maggie's wholehearted responsiveness to his every suggestion acted upon him like the strongest aphrodisiac. Reciprocating in kind to his every touch, every caress, she had unconditionally surrendered to him, and in turn, he had unconditionally surrendered to her.

In the end Maggie had cried out his name in tones of amazement and disbelief while in the throes of utter release. Her cries of pleasure, and the speculation that she had never experienced such an all-consuming release, had heightened his own satisfaction.

At thirty-five, Mitch was far from a novice in the art of sensual pleasures. Yet, for all his worldly experience, never had he known—lived through, died through—such an intense, mind-and-body-shattering sexual encounter, as he had with Maggie.

His body was still pulsating in reaction to the gut-wrenching intensity of his climax. His heart was still thumping, his nerves still thrumming like a vibrating guitar string, his breathing still shallow and irregular.

Damn...he loved it, loved it so much, he replayed the scene in bits and pieces in his pleasure-addled mind.

His gaze surveying Maggie's sleep-softened features, Mitch relived the taste of her creamy skin, the tickle of her eyelashes against his lips, the moist sweetness of her mouth, her tongue, joined in carnal hunger with his.

His chest tightening, Mitch slid his gaze to her hair, spread like strands of living flames in wild disarray against the pillow—*his* pillow. And it had been his fingers, coiling, curling, grasping those strands that had caused that tale-telling disarray.

A sudden dryness parched his throat. Mitch's gaze moved on to her satiny shoulders and lower, to her breasts. Their deliciously tempting tips were still tight and hard from the attention lavished upon them by his tongue, his greedily sucking lips.

Desire reawakening his body, Mitch trailed his gaze lower still. He followed the neat indentation of her slim waist, the alluring flare of her hips, the gentle roundness of her belly, the parted juncture of her thighs.

Sweet heaven.

Mitch closed his eyes. Perspiration sheened his forehead. He was quivering, actually quivering in response to the passion roaring through him.

With every fiber of his being, Mitch wanted, needed to experience that heaven again.

Sliding his rigid body down the enticing

length of hers, he lowered his head to bestow the most adoring and intimate of kisses on the portal of her sweet heaven.

Maggie roused to an aching, fiery sensation in the core of her being. Sensual energy recharged her depleted body. Not fully awake, but luxuriating in the new sensation, she moved in sinuous response, parting her thighs and arching her hips.

Soft laughter, followed by a quick, hot caress against the most sensitive part of her femininity brought her fully awake, shockingly aware.

"Mitch…no," she protested, stiffening.

"Maggie…yes," he murmured, delving deeper.

She wanted to resist, felt compelled to resist, but the sensations swirling through her from his ministrations defeated her resistance, turned it into raging desire. Writhing, helpless within the grip of erotic pleasure, she grasped his head, dug her fingers into his hair, arched her hips high and gave herself up to the hungry fire of his mouth.

Tension unlike anything Maggie had ever experienced wound tighter and tighter until, gasping, pleading, fearing she'd go mad from the pleasure, the tension snapped and a torrent of even more intense pleasure cascaded through her.

Her breathing labored, Maggie lay exhausted. At least she thought she was exhausted, beyond the slightest movement, until she heard the faint but unmistakable noise of tearing foil. Mitch surged up over her and into her, further intensifying the diminishing pulsations.

It was fast, and furious. And to Maggie's utter disbelief, she once again went soaring into ecstasy, and promptly into the enfolding blanket of slumber.

"Maggie... Are you dead?"

Mitch's soft tones roused her consciousness, his teasing aroused her amusement.

"Yes."

"Too bad." His voice held silent laughter. "I guess I'll have to drink the coffee I brought for you."

"Coffee?" Maggie pried open her eyes to see him standing next to the bed, a cup in each hand. He looked devastating, clad in nothing but faded jeans that rode his slim hips. "Caffeinated?"

"What else?"

Inhaling the aroma rising from the steaming brew, Maggie groaned in appreciation as she levered herself up, then yelped with the realization that she was stark naked.

"Will you hand me my blouse?" she asked, yanking the sheet up to her neck.

"Why?" he drawled, grinning at the fierce frown she'd produced. "I've seen...and tasted...it all."

"I could say the same of you, yet you're covered," she muttered. "Mitch, please," she pleaded, feeling her face, her entire body grow warm with embarrassment at the flood of memories, her abandonment... How long ago?

"Oh, all right, Little Ms. Modest," he grouched, his silvery eyes gleaming with amusement.

Sighing with relief, Maggie clamped the sheet under her arms. Wriggling into a sitting position, she watched him as he set the cups on the nightstand and turned to a chair, where her neatly folded clothes lay draped over the high back, obviously placed there by Mitch.

"What time is it, anyway?" she asked, quickly shrugging into the blouse he tossed to her.

"Ten-twenty," he said, handing a cup to her. "Why, are you going somewhere?"

Cradling the cup in her palms, Maggie raised it to her lips and took a careful sip of the aromatic brew. "Hmm, lovely," she murmured, taking another sip before answering his question. "If you'll recall, I told Karla and Ben I'd join them if it didn't get too late…which, of course, it now is."

"Does not being able to join them bother you?"

Giving serious concentration to her caffeine intake, Maggie wasn't looking at him. But the tight edge to his tone snagged her attention, drew her gaze to his face. His expression was closed and every bit as tight as his voice.

"Bother me?" she repeated, frowning. "No, it doesn't bother me. Why should it?"

Mitch's lips curved into what she felt sure was supposed to be a smile. It had more the look of a grimace. "Come on, Maggie," he said chidingly. "What is one supposed to think? Ben's been hanging around here since he arrived. He escorted you out to dinner, Lord knows how many times the last two weeks. And even though he has kindly included Karla in on the outings, it's obvious to anyone with eyes in their head that he's attracted, one might even say extremely attracted, to you."

Maggie nearly choked on her coffee. Fortunately, she managed to swallow before bursting into laughter.

"What the hell's so damn funny?" Anger flashed in his eyes.

"You," she said, stifling her mirth. "And your all-seeing but clouded vision."

"Meaning?" Mitch demanded, bristling.

He looked so affronted, so rattled by his failure to intimidate her, Maggie had to fight another gurgle of laughter. "Meaning," she said, sweetly, "you obviously missed the real truth."

He actually growled. "Explain."

"Ben is not attracted to me, Mitch." She heaved a dramatic sigh. "He's crazy about Karla."

He looked both stunned and shocked. "But... Good Lord, Maggie, she's pregnant."

"No!" Maggie exclaimed, widening her eyes in a parody of astonishment. "How did it... Well, I know how, but... When did this happen?"

"Cute." Mitch somehow managed to sound annoyed, amused and relieved at one and the same time. "And you don't mind...about Ben's interest in her?"

"Why should I mind?" She shook her head. "I mean, other than a natural concern about whether Ben's interest in her is genuine."

"Understandable, of course, but..." He

shrugged. "I thought you were attracted to him."

Now it was Maggie who felt affronted, really insulted. They had just had sex...which, to her at any rate, had seemed more like making love. Could Mitch seriously believe she would go to bed with one man while feeling attracted to another?

To Maggie, it was patently obvious that that was exactly what Mitch believed. Damn his hide.

"I see," she said, her cool tone reflecting an inner chill of pain. Setting her empty cup on the night table, she clutched at the sides of her blouse with trembling fingers and slid her sheet-draped legs over the edge of the mattress. "If you'd turn your back, please," she said, not looking at him, "I'd like to use the bathroom."

"What's wrong?"

"I have to leave," she muttered, staring at the carpet, and absently noting it was plush, a deep chocolate brown. "It's getting late."

"It's not that late. Maggie, what's wrong?"

"I told you," she said to the carpet. "I must go. I need to clean up and dress."

"Look at me, Maggie." It wasn't a request, but a direct order.

From the boss to the... Maggie shook her

head in denial of the ugly word that sprang into her mind.

"Damn it, Maggie," he exploded, stepping closer to her. "What's wrong?"

She saw his feet crush the carpet before she felt his hands grab her shoulders to pull her upright. Suddenly furious, she jerked her head back and glared at him.

"I'm mad as hell, that's what's wrong."

"What?" Mitch looked bewildered. "Mad about what?"

Chin tilted at an aggressive angle, Maggie lashed out at him. "How dare you insinuate that I'd go to bed with one man, while feeling attracted to another?"

"I didn't... I..."

"You did." Exasperated, irritated, Maggie raked him with a withering look. She hadn't felt so incensed since June, when she'd discovered that note. Inside her mind, she was no longer seeing just Mitch, but Todd and every other insensitive male she had ever met.

"Maggie...I swear I don't know what you're talking about." His hands tightened on her shoulders. She shrugged out of his hold and sidestepped away from him.

"Men." On a roll, she practically spat the word at him. "You're all alike, taking what you want from whomever you want, without a thought or care for any pain or mental damage you might inflict.''

''What pain?'' Mitch gave her a helpless look. ''What mental damage have I inflicted—'' He broke off, his eyes narrowing. ''Who did this to you…hurt you?'' he asked—demanded—in icy tones. ''Was it Ben?''

''Ben? Again?'' Maggie threw her hands in the air. ''I told you I'm not interested in Ben that way.''

''Then who?'' Mitch persisted. ''And don't hand me that bull about me insinuating anything unsavory about you. I meant no such thing. It's more than that…much more. Isn't it? You're attacking me for something some other son of a bitch did. Aren't you?''

Maggie sighed, deflating as fast as she had blown up. She had overreacted, and she knew it. ''Yes,'' she admitted, hastening to add, ''but I did feel as though you were casting aspersions on my character.''

''I wasn't.'' His voice was hard with conviction. ''He hurt you very badly?''

She smiled with wry self-knowledge. ''He hurt my pride,'' she confessed, her face flaming as she suddenly realized she was standing there stark naked from the waist down. If she hadn't felt so vulnerable, it might have been funny, she with only her chest covered, Mitch with only his...bottom concealed. "May I get dressed now?" she said, shifting uncomfortably.

"You're not going to tell me, are you?"

"Mitch, I feel like a fool, standing here half-dressed like this," she snapped, patience wearing thin. "Will you please point me toward the bathroom."

"Right there." He indicated a door on the far wall. "But I expect some answers when you're finished."

Dream on, mister. Maggie didn't bother verbalizing the thought. Scooping her clothes from the chair, she dashed for the bathroom.

Twenty minutes later, after making free with his shower in the luxurious black-and-white-tiled bathroom, Maggie strode back into the bedroom. Her confidence was restored by the armor of being fully clothed.

Mitch, on the other hand, apparently felt well protected by the indomitable force of his personality. He sat sprawled in a wing chair, still clad in nothing but the jeans, unbuttoned at the waist.

The sensuous sight of him had Maggie reeling from an erotic blow to her senses.

She sucked in a steadying breath.

He smiled, slow and sexy. "You look fantastic…but I liked you better the other way, with your gorgeous hair all wild and tangled, and your lips red and pouty from my kisses, and your beautiful green eyes shadowed by passion."

Good heavens. Maggie's legs went weak. Heat seared through her, tingling the tips of her breasts, drawing moisture from the core of her being. It was crazy, sheer madness. Nevertheless, she wanted him. Again. So soon.

He held out a hand. "Come to me, Maggie," he murmured in a low siren-song voice.

Every living cell in her body urged her to obey his whispered plea, relive the ecstasy to be found in his embrace, his possession.

She actually took one step toward him, before common sense came to her rescue, warning her that if she surrendered to him again, she'd be a goner, defenseless against his potent kisses. She shook her head in denial, of him and herself. Until she felt certain she could trust him…

"Maggie, trust me," he crooned, as if he could read the turmoil of her conflicting thoughts.

She shook her head again. "I told you before, I don't trust any man. And now, since we—" she glanced at the rumpled bed, then quickly looked away "—I no longer trust myself."

"He really did a number on you, didn't he?" His voice harsh with disgust, Mitch sprang from the chair to confront her, his hands planted on his slim hips.

"Yes," she admitted, holding her ground, facing him with challenge. "But, you see, I allowed it by doing a number on myself," she conceded.

"How?"

Maggie smiled, faint and self-deprecatingly. "By convincing myself I was in love with him."

Speculation silvered his eyes. "You weren't in love with him...whoever the hell he is?"

She squared her shoulders and raised her chin. "No, I wasn't in love with him," she confessed. "I was feeling desperate. I was tired of the upwardly mobile mania. My biological clock was running. I longed for a child, a family, a man I could trust to provide those things." She shrugged. "It was easy to convince myself I was in love."

"You wanted marriage," he concluded.

"Yes, I wanted marriage," she said, a wry smile twisting her lips. "And I believed I was going to get what I wanted," she added, feeling a need to at last purge herself, her mind of the humiliating experience. "Everything was arranged. Then, two weeks before the big event, he eloped with his employer's daughter, and heir. He left me a note, and a mess to clean up.''

''The bastard,'' Mitch growled.

''That's precisely what I said.'' She smiled. ''I went wacky for a while. I slashed my damned wedding gown into ribbons, quit my job, rented out my apartment and simply loaded my car and started driving. I finally wound up here, in Deadwood.''

''I'm glad you did.''

''I'm sure you are,'' she said dryly, shooting a pointed look at the bed. ''And now I'll be on my way.'' Swinging around, she headed for the door.

''Wait a damned minute,'' he said, his hand clasping her arm to stop her in her tracks, turning her to face him. ''Where are you going?''

''Home, to my bed...'' She smiled, almost.

''I'd rather you slept here, in *my* bed.'' His soft voice enticed her senses.

Maggie drew a slow, steadying breath. ''I don't think so,'' she said, shaking her head. ''I lost my head there for a while, but it's back in place now. This—'' she flicked a hand at the bed ''—won't happen again.''

''Not even if you find you can trust me?'' he asked, raising a hand to cup her face.

Maggie's breathing went haywire. He was going to kiss her. She knew he was going to kiss her. She knew as well that she should stop him, step away from him…run away from him. She neither stopped him nor ran. She parted her lips for him.

Mitch's mouth was gentle on hers, sweet, undemanding, demoralizing.

"Maggie?" He lifted his head to stare into her eyes. "If you find you can trust me?"

She swallowed and pulled her scattered senses together. "Maybe. We'll see."

"Good enough." Releasing his hold on her arm, and her face, Mitch stepped back. "I'll follow you home."

"No." Maggie shook her head. "That's not necessary."

He sighed. "Don't argue, Maggie. Just give me a few minutes to get dressed."

Maggie didn't argue, but as soon as he had crossed the room and entered the bathroom, she called, "Don't forget that fax for your brother."

Then she ran.

Exasperating woman. Fumbling with the top snap on his jeans, silently cursing, Mitch pushed open the bathroom door and strode to the clothes closet, determined to pull on a shirt and shoes and tear after Maggie.

He was stamping into buff-toned desert boots when he heard a car start up in the employees' parking lot.

"Dammit," he muttered, kicking off the boots. No point in going after her now. Letting the boots lie where they fell, he turned to the nightstand to collect their coffee cups, and stopped still at the sight of the rumpled bed.

A shiver-inducing thrill, immediately followed by a searing streak of heat, shot through him at the vivid recollection of the activity that had caused the wild disorder of bedding.

Lord, she was magnificent, this woman who had presented a challenge to him from the first day she had walked into his office. Was it really only a little over two weeks ago? Mitch asked himself. It seemed more like months, or years that he had spent watching Maggie, learning her mannerisms, her particular personality traits, listening for the sound of her voice, her laughter…wanting her.

And now that he had tasted the fullness of her, tapped the depths of her sensuality, reveled in her surrender, Mitch instinctively feared he would never again live to see a day dawn that he did not want to be with her, in and out of bed.

It was a sobering consideration. It was a mind-

and life-altering thought, most especially since Maggie, the woman who didn't trust any man, just might decide on the spur of any moment to cut and run.

Maggie was afraid. She was afraid to trust not only men, but herself. Because one lapse in her judgment had allowed her to lead herself down the proverbial garden path.

And yet, by his observation—and he had made almost a science of observing her—she had revealed not only a quick wit and sharp intelligence, but a warm, caring personality. She showed genuine affection, with a strong strain of protectiveness toward Karla...which he highly approved of. In addition, everyone she had come in contact with in the casino appeared to like and respect her.

All of which was a clear indication to Mitch that the cool, savvy, challenging, almost militant front she presented was simply that—a self-protective facade.

And beneath that facade was a many-faceted woman, a woman confident and comfortable wearing many of life's hats.

Maggie wanted a child, a family life...

The matter needed more serious thought.

Grabbing up the cups, Mitch left the bedroom and headed for the kitchen. If he was going to engage in some mental and emotional probing and come up with some viable solutions, he needed caffeine, lots of caffeine.

By 3:00 a.m. he was tired but wide awake. His hair was ruffled from repeated raking of fingers and he fairly sloshed with the two pots of coffee he had drunk. But his mental and emotional state was resolved as he stumbled down to his office to at last send the fax to his brother.

As impossible and improbable as it seemed to him, and after much soul-searching, Mitch had finally faced the singularly amazing fact that he was in love with Maggie Reynolds. He was deeply, irrevocably and forever-after in love with her.

Who would have thought? Certainly not Mitch. He had long since decided that love, romantic love, was for, well…romantics, of which he was not one.

But there it was, romantic love, in all its gut-wrenching glory, figuratively laughing its ass off at him. Okay, let it laugh. Better yet, hopefully, he'd laugh along.

But now, Mitch acknowledged, his work was really cut out for him. For now, he had to not only prove to Maggie that she could trust him, but love him back in return.

It was enough to make a strong, iron-willed man weep.

Of course, Mitch wasn't into weeping over his troubles, or anything else. He never had been. He was into taking whatever action was required to remedy the situation.

With his eyelids heavy, but his brain alert on caffeine, Mitch retraced his steps to his bedroom. Shucking out of his clothes, he crawled naked into the tangled bedding and set about devising a strategy to lure Maggie back into the bed next to him…for the rest of her natural life.

Nine

It was raining, hard. Fortunately, it was Saturday. At least she didn't have to go to work and beard her personal dragon in his den, so to speak, Maggie thought as she dragged her weary, sleep-denied body from the bed. She had a headache, most likely from the battering her brain had taken throughout the long night of mental taxation. She also ached in some, no, a lot of very delicate places.

And it was all thanks to her personal, bedrock-hard dragon, she reflected. She now had firsthand knowledge of how very hard, and gentle, Mitch could be.

What to do? What to do?

Sick and tired of the endless question, Maggie started a pot of coffee. Then she headed for the bathroom to beat her protesting body parts into submission with a hot shower.

Fifteen minutes later, she felt marginally better, so far as her aching muscles went. Dressed in jeans and an oversize Penn State University sweatshirt, Maggie sat curled up on the kitchen window seat, a steaming cup of coffee warming her cradling hands.

Three sips of the brew made her feel almost human. Perhaps some food. Maggie made a face. Perhaps not. So, okay, she advised herself. Drink the coffee and think it through.

Then again, what was to think about? She had felt an immediate attraction to Mitch, an attraction she had thought was purely physical in nature. Think again.

Mitch was scrupulously honest, not only fair but generous with his employees, and genuinely concerned for their well-being. In retrospect, Maggie had to laugh at her original suspicions about Mitch being the father of Karla's baby. He actually acted more like Karla's father, monitoring her increasing condition, making sure she ate right and wasn't overdoing the office work, insisting she stay off her feet when her ankles swelled.

Maggie had quickly come to appreciate Mitch's sense of humor, revealed in the teasing gleam that lit his eyes, the occasional droll remark, the laughter that rang out, free and clear of any malicious content.

And Mitch was fantastic in bed. The errant thought induced a delicious tingle inside Maggie. Good heavens, she never dreamed she could feel the sensations she had experienced in his bed. Of course, she was sadly inexperienced, since Todd had been her one and only lover...and he had hardly aroused her, never mind set her on fire. For Maggie, sex with Todd had been a functional exchange, uninspired and finished quickly.

With Mitch... Maggie sighed. With Mitch the physical act had been an enlightenment, a feast of sensual delights, a shared journey through exotic realms.

Every living cell in her body cried out to share that journey with Mitch again. Share the closeness, the laughter, the passion, the feeling of being joyously alive.

By her third cup of coffee, Maggie admitted that she could very easily fall in love with

Mitch…if in fact she hadn't already fallen in love with him. If she dared.

But Mitch had a thing about trust.

Maggie winced. She had a thing about trust, too. Her thing being that she had good reason to doubt the sincerity of any man's avowed trustworthiness.

What to do? What to do?

Maggie was back at square one.

Hugging her knees, she stared out the window at the pouring rain, noticing that autumn had come to South Dakota. The leaves on the trees behind the house, colorful mere days before, were drying. Many had already fallen to the ground. There was a chill in the air she could feel through the windowpane.

Maybe it was time to hit the trail, go home to Philadelphia before winter set in.

She sighed again. The shame of her situation was that she really liked being here. She liked the town, the surrounding terrain. She liked her work. She liked her apartment. She liked Karla, and the other employees she had come to know over the previous two weeks. And, despite her initial misgivings, she liked Mitch, the man.

The man wanted her.

And she wanted him.

A part of her demanded she give it time, explore the possibility of a workable and satisfying relationship with Mitch. Another part of her, the wary part, urged her to pack up and take off before she got hurt again.

But she couldn't go, at least not yet, Maggie told the wary part. She had to stay, wanted to stay until after Karla's baby was born. So she'd stay...awhile.

But she'd have to play it cool, Maggie told herself. Resisting Mitch wouldn't be easy, but she would have to keep him at arm's length. And maybe, with any luck, she might discover that she could place her trust in him.

One could always hope.

Maggie took her tired body, and her hope, back to bed.

The phone woke her late in the afternoon. It was still raining, and almost dark.

"Where have you been hiding all day?" Karla's cheery voice brought full wakefulness.

"Right here," Maggie said, covering a yawn with her hand. "I was having a nap."

"Did Mitch keep you at it very late?"

A loaded question if Maggie ever heard one. She played it straight. "Not too late," she answered, her tone neutral. "I left around ten-thirty." Which was true. "But I didn't sleep well, so I went back to bed.'' Also true. ''Did you and Ben have a nice evening?''

A pause, then Karla said, ''Oh, yes, we had a lovely dinner, and then we just talked.''

''May I ask what about?''

''Sure,'' Karla said, her voice light, happy. ''I'll tell you everything over supper.''

Maggie smiled, and pushed a swath of hair from her eyes. ''We're having supper together?''

''Yep, chicken and salad, and it's almost done.'' Karla laughed. ''You have twenty minutes to get up, get dressed and get yourself down here.''

Maggie produced a not entirely fake groan. ''Nag.''

Karla laughed again. ''Did I mention that the chicken is in a pasta dish…with mushrooms and other good stuff?''

Laughing to herself, Maggie threw back the covers. ''Start the coffee, I'll be down in fifteen.''

''Oh, that was so-o-o good,'' Maggie complimented the cook, sighing with repletion as she set her napkin aside. ''Where did you find the recipe?''

''I'm so glad it turned out right, and that you liked it,'' Karla said, smiling with pleasure for the compliment. "I got it from one of those TV cooking shows."

"It was wonderful," Maggie said, feeling stuffed, and curious. "So, was your dinner last night as good?"

"Yes." Karla nodded. "But later was better."

"Later?" Maggie prompted.

Karla nodded, looking shy. "We...Ben and I came back here after dinner to talk."

Alarm flared inside Maggie, concern for her innocent friend. Ben was a mature man, after all, a virile, healthy male. "And...er, what did you talk about?"

"Us...Ben and me." Karla's cheeks bloomed with becoming pink. "He said...he's in love with me."

"Karla..." The alarm bells were clanging, and Maggie didn't know how to proceed, other than directly. "He didn't...you didn't...?"

"Go to bed with him?" Karla said it for her. "No, I didn't. I wanted to," she quickly added. "I know I'm in love with him—Ben's so wonderful. And I really wanted to make love with him before he had to leave but..."

"But?" Maggie repeated, fearing that the couple had tried but that Karla had found it uncomfortable.

"He wouldn't."

The simple statement rocked Maggie's precepts of the male gender. *"He wouldn't?"*

"No." Karla pouted. "He said he was afraid he'd hurt me or the baby."

"Well, good for him," Maggie said, breathing a silent sigh of relief. "Is he still planning to come back here and be with you through the birth?"

"Yes." The pink in her cheeks deepened to red. "And he promised he'd make up for last night...after we're married."

"He proposed?"

"Not really." She giggled. "He just said we're getting married, that we'd do it as soon as it could be arranged. But he had to go back to the ranch first and talk to his boss."

What was wrong with the telephone? Maggie wondered with cynical suspicion. Not wanting to upset Karla, she kept her mouth shut.

"Oh, Maggie, I'm so happy. I couldn't wait another minute to tell you. That's why I called." She laughed. "And, you'll be surprised to hear, I was so happy, I called my folks, too. Told them everything. They're coming to Deadwood the week before my due date to be with me when the baby comes."

"Oh, Karla, I'm so glad you called them. And I am happy for you," Maggie said, jumping up to hug her friend, glad she had kept her suspicions to herself.

"Have dinner with me." It was Wednesday, and the third time that week Mitch had asked that same question. Over a week and a half had elapsed since the memorable night they had been together. And though she had maintained a pleasant, outwardly friendly demeanor, Maggie had kept a cool and deliberate distance between them.

"Mitch, I..." Maggie began.

"Wait," Mitch interrupted her, certain she was about to refuse him, again. "Just dinner, Maggie, no strings, no pressure for anything more. I promise."

"I don't know." She hesitated, her gaze steady on his, her eyes revealing an inner conflict.

Encouraged, Mitch forged ahead. "Maggie, it's only dinner. I'm inviting you to have a meal with me, not an orgy," he said, even though, with the constant memory of those incredible hours they'd spent together tormenting him, an orgy sounded pretty good to him. Especially considering how difficult he was finding it to keep his hands off her.

Maggie didn't frown, or go stiff and cold with rejection. She laughed. More encouraging still.

"If I say please?"

"Well…" She smiled. "If you behave yourself."

With a sorrowful expression, he placed a hand on his chest over his heart. "You wound me."

"I seriously doubt it," she drawled, arching a brow and looking suspicious. "Where?"

Mitch knew exactly what she was asking. "Not in my apartment, if that's what's worrying you."

"It was," she admitted.

"But we were so good together, so…" Mitch caught himself up short, but it was too late, the impassioned words were out, dangling there in the sudden silence.

Maggie didn't respond or even react. She simply sat there, still as death, staring at him.

Damned fool, Mitch berated himself. He'd screwed up, big time, and it would serve him right if she told him to take a flying leap off a high cliff. He knew how she felt, knew she didn't trust him.

The results of winging it, he supposed. After crawling back into bed the night they had been together, Mitch had scrapped the notion of forming a strategy to win Maggie's trust, and eventually her love. He'd decided to just be himself. For if she couldn't come to trust him, love him, for what and who he was, the whole thing would be pointless. Maybe he should have gone with a strategy. Too late now, he thought, his path was set.

"Maggie, I'm sorry. Not about us being good together. I'm not sorry about that, because we were, more than merely good, more like fantastic. But I am sorry for bringing it up now, when I know you don't want to discuss it."

"You're right, I don't wish to discuss it." She moved her shoulders in a minishrug. "But you're also right about being good together—we were."

"But...then why..."

The simple act of raising her hand silenced him. "I don't know where you're coming from, what you want from me—" a wry smile brushed her lips "—other than sex."

"It was more than sex, Maggie." Mitch paused, then admitted with blunt honesty, "Okay, to begin with it was the sexual attraction... I felt it, and you felt it, too." He gave her a hard stare. "Didn't you?"

"Yes." She met his stare with commendable directness. "And it rattled me."

He smiled. "I know."

"It still does."

His smile softened. "I know. That's why you've been keeping your distance from me, even though the attraction is still there, just as strong."

She nodded in agreement but didn't return his smile.

"Then, don't you think we should explore this attraction? We could spend time together, away from this office and get to know each other. Not in bed," he quickly assured her, "even though I'll admit I want that, too."

"You're suggesting a platonic relationship?" Maggie's voice and expression were skeptical.

"For a while...hopefully a short while...until we see if we have anything else going for us."

Maggie studied him, quiet, pensive. Too long.

"Well, what do you say?" he said, impatience riding him. "I did promise I'd behave."

She sighed, smiled and said, "Okay."

And not a second too soon, because Mitch couldn't hold his breath any longer.

"I loved that movie," Maggie exclaimed, laughing. "It was so off-the-wall."

"I'll say." Mitch laughed with her. "You can't get more off-the-wall than the Frankenstein monster dancing and singing 'Putting on the Ritz.'"

Maggie nodded. "I must have seen it a dozen times," she confessed.

Mitch grinned. "Me, too."

His grin sent a shiver down Maggie's spine. Wrapping her trembling fingers around her coffee cup, she raised it to her lips. Dinner was over. She had enjoyed every bite of the meal; she had enjoyed Mitch's company more, even though he did send hot and cold chills through her.

Ever since Mitch had picked her up at the apartment—he wouldn't hear of her meeting him somewhere, then driving home alone afterward—his behavior had been above reproach. He had opened the car door for her, usurped the restaurant host by holding her chair for her, and had broken the initial awkward silence by recounting amusing anecdotes.

Nervous at the outset, she had been nearly overwhelmed by the sheer masculine attraction of him. She yearned for him, and the yearning both scared and annoyed her, rendering her almost incapable of anything but the most monosyllabic responses to his attempts at conversation.

But her vocal ice was broken the first time he

made her laugh. From then on, talking got easier. The evening became less a strain and surprisingly enlightening.

Maggie would never have dreamed that two people from different parts of the country with completely different lifestyles could have so much in common. And yet they did.

She had already known, of course, that they both preferred caffeinated coffee. But, over the course of the meal, she had discovered they shared a passion for sunsets over sunrises, mind-teasing mystery stories, cheeseburgers and pasta. Their mutual appreciation of zany comedy was the latest discovery.

"I want children."

Mitch's bald statement startled Maggie out of her things-in-common amazement. "What?"

"I said, I want children." He shrugged. "I just thought I'd make that clear up front."

"Okay," she said warily. "And your point being…?"

"You told me…that night…that you had convinced yourself you were in love, because you wanted to step off the career treadmill, have a home life, a family. I wanted you to know that I want those same things."

So had Todd, or so he'd said, Maggie thought, her mellow mood rapidly dissipating. But all

she'd been to Todd was a convenient bed part-
ner, until something better came along. The old
resentment flared, fueled by new resentment for
Mitch, for ruining the pleasant evening.

"I...ah, think I'd like to go home now," she
said, her voice tight, her body trembling.

"Maggie, I'm not him." Mitch's voice was
harsh with frustration.

"I know that." Carefully setting her cup in
the saucer, she folded her hands in her lap.

"Then cut me some slack." He raked long
fingers through his neatly brushed hair. "Dammit, Maggie, you're driving me nuts. I want you,
you know that. But I want more than a couple
nights in bed with you, or a couple months. I
want it all. I know I promised not to pressure
you, but..." He broke off, cursing under his
breath. "I'm bungling this, I know. But, you see,
I've never been in this position before. I've
never been in love before."

Love. Maggie blinked. Love? Impossible.
Wasn't it? They barely knew each other. Yet,
she had felt the same emotional stirrings. Had
felt she could easily fall in love with him if, that
is, she didn't already love him.

Maggie was very afraid that she was in love
with him. And it scared the hell out of her. He
scared the hell out of her. What if she were to

commit herself to him, and then... No. She shook her head. She wouldn't be able to bear it if Mitch were to walk out on her.

"I want to go home," she repeated in an agonized whisper, denying an inner longing to find a home in his arms.

"Maggie, trust me, please," he implored her, his voice raw. "I won't hurt you."

"I...need time."

"How much time?"

"I...don't know."

"All right. Take all the time you need. I'll wait." He sighed. "I have no other choice."

The atmosphere in the office the next day was rather strained, although Mitch made a gallant effort at maintaining a normal workday appearance.

Though she tried to emulate his in-office professional attitude, Maggie was miserable. Her heart was torn between the desire to take a chance, grab hold of Mitch, accept whatever he offered, and the chilling fear of again losing everything.

They circled around each other like two magnetized metals, fighting the attraction drawing them together.

Off in her own rosy world of planning a future

with Ben and the child she was carrying, Karla was unconscious of the drama being played out between Mitch and Maggie.

On Friday, Maggie sighed in relief, tension easing as lunchtime approached. It was Karla's last day of work. With Mitch's ready approval, Maggie had planned a surprise baby shower for her during the lunch break. He had even bent the rules a little, not only by extending the lunch hour for the other female office workers on the second floor, but by shifting break periods for the women friends of Karla's on the casino floor and in the restaurant, so they could join the party. He had also made arrangements for the restaurant kitchen staff to cater the affair and provide a decorated cake.

By prearrangement, Mitch called Karla into the office ten minutes before noon. The moment the door closed behind her, Maggie went into action. Ushering the tiptoeing women and servers into the outer office, they got to work, stringing streamers, positioning a pink-and-blue-striped umbrella, setting out the food and drinks.

Within fifteen minutes, everything was in place. Maggie alerted Mitch with a short buzz of the intercom. Karla exited his office to cries of "Surprise!" Flabbergasted, she laughed, then burst into tears. Shaking his head at the mysterious emotions of pregnant females, Mitch beat a hasty retreat, making himself scarce by doing a regular sweep of the premises.

It was great fun. There was a lot of laughter and teasing, mingled with a few scattered tears. When it came time to open the pile of gifts set before her, Karla rummaged in her desk for a pair of scissors. Finding none, she glanced at Maggie.

"I think there's a pair in Mitch's office. Try the top-center desk drawer."

Maggie zipped into the office and to his desk. She found the small pair of scissors, but that wasn't all she found. Shoved into one corner was a ring. It wasn't just any old ring, but what appeared to Maggie to be an obviously expensive and elaborate engagement ring.

Frowning, she removed the scissors, closed the drawer and returned to the party. But a niggling concern dampened her spirit.

Although the party lasted less than two hours, it seemed to drag much longer for Maggie. It ended when Mitch strode back into the office. Taking their cue, the employees drifted back to work, the women from the restaurant taking the food and drink carts with them. Maggie began clearing away wrapping paper and stacking the gifts.

"You two might as well call it a day," Mitch said, smiling into Karla's flushed, bemused face. "I've asked Frank to come help you carry your loot to the car."

"Oh, but..." Karla began in token protest.

Troubled by the possible connotations concerning the ring she had seen in his desk, Maggie stayed silent.

"No buts," he decreed. "The excitement has tired you. Go home and rest." He ended the discussion by walking into his office and shutting the door.

Frank arrived with another security guard in tow, and between the four of them, they managed to transfer the gifts to Maggie's car in one trip.

It wasn't until after they were in Karla's apartment, the gifts piled on the sofa and Karla settled in a chair, that Maggie tentatively broached the subject of the ring.

"Oh, that." Karla made a face.

"It looked like an engagement ring," Maggie ventured. "A very expensive engagement ring."

"It is...or was," Karla said, nodding. "Mitch was engaged for a few months to the daughter of a prominent local family. The wedding date was set, but..." She shrugged.

Maggie felt a chill. Not another man who

made commitments, then broke them at will? She had to know.

"What happened?"

Karla sighed. "It was a misunderstanding on Miss Crane's part."

Miss Crane? The name rang a sharp peal in Maggie's memory. She'd taken a call from a Natalie Crane, demanding to speak to Mitch. And Maggie remembered his harsh order for her to get rid of the woman. The chill intensified inside her.

"I felt terrible about it," Karla continued.

Maggie frowned. "What did you have to do with it?"

"It happened right after I found out I was pregnant," she explained. "I was upset, afraid to tell my parents. I didn't know where to turn." She sighed again. "So I cried my troubles out to Mitch…literally. Trying to comfort me, he held me in his arms and let me cry on his shoulder. We didn't hear Miss Crane enter the office. She saw me in his arms, heard me mention the baby and naturally assumed the worst. She threw the ring at him and ran out."

"But…surely he went after her…explained the situation?" Maggie asked.

"No." Karla shook her head. "I offered to go see her, explain the circumstances, but he wouldn't let me. He said it was over, and that was that.''

''I see,'' Maggie murmured, very much afraid that what she saw was the picture of a man, a bedrock-hard man, who could discard women as easily as he could a rumpled shirt. The very idea caused a sharp pain in her heart.

After coaxing Karla to lie down and rest, Maggie climbed the stairs to her apartment, where she curled up on the window seat to do some heavy thinking.

She loved him, Maggie acknowledged. And this time, the emotion was for real—it wouldn't hurt so badly if it weren't. But fear and trepidation riddled her thinking. An impulse to hit the trail was strong and compelling. At the same time, an equally strong impulse urged her to stay, confront Mitch with her knowledge of his previous engagement, hear whatever he had to say for himself.

But she was so afraid to trust again. If she were to have her trust thrown back in her face, she knew that something inside her would shatter.

Her ruminations were interrupted by Mitch's phone call later that afternoon.

''Hi, is our little mother okay after all the tears and excitement?''

"Yes," Maggie answered, her stomach lurching at the sound of his voice, a longing for him tugging at her emotions. "I think she's having a nap."

"Good. How about you and I having dinner?"

"Mitch...I..." Maggie paused to swallow against the emotional tightness in her throat.

"Maggie, what is it?" His tone had an edge of anxiety. "What's wrong?"

In that instant, Maggie made a decision. She was tired of running. She had to know, even if the knowing squashed her emotionally. "We must...talk."

"I'll be right over," he said at once.

"No." Maggie gave a sharp shake of her head, even though he couldn't see her. "I don't want Karla to start wondering why you're here. I'll go there... You're still at the office?"

"Yes, but..."

"I'll be there in a few minutes."

A few minutes. Her words echoed in Maggie's head all the way to the casino. Within a few short minutes her whole world could change.

Mitch was standing by the window, waiting for her. His expression was somber, his body rigid with tension.

"What's this all about, Maggie?"

Maggie crossed directly to his desk, slid open the top drawer. "This afternoon, quite by accident, I saw this." She lifted the ring with two fingers.

"It is, or was an engagement ring," he said, walking toward her to pluck the bauble from her fingers. "Rather garish and ostentatious, isn't it?"

Since that had been her own private opinion, Maggie had to agree. "Yes."

"What about it?" With a careless flick of his fingers, he tossed it back into the drawer and closed it.

"I asked Karla about it."

"Of course." He smiled, a wry twist of his lips. "And immediately jumped to conclusions about me. None of them favorable. Right?"

At his cool tone, Maggie suddenly recalled Karla's words, telling her about Mitch's thoughts on trust. And she knew, without his spelling it out, that he was daring her to test it, test him...while simultaneously, he would test her.

"I'm afraid so," she confessed, facing him squarely. "I've been burned before, Mitch."

"Not by me," he pointed out in hard tones.

"Yet," she retaliated.

His chest expanded, then contracted on a sigh. "What the hell do you expect me to do? I'm sure Karla told you the sorry details. What more is there to say?"

"You tossed Miss Crane aside as easily as you tossed that ring into the drawer," she cried accusingly.

"She didn't trust me," he retorted angrily. "So why should I have given a damn?"

The trust thing. Still, something didn't ring right to Maggie. A question niggled. "But I just indicated a doubt in your trust. Where's the difference?"

"I love *you*," he declared, in less than loverlike tones. "I never loved her. As I believe I already told you, I've never loved any other woman."

"Oh," Maggie murmured, feeling confused and extremely flattered at one and the same time. "And loving me, you're willing to be patient with my doubts?"

"Hell, yes," he said, hauling her into his arms. "Maggie, you've been hurt. I understand that. And you're cautious. I understand that, too. But I love you. And I want you. In bed. Out of bed. In my life. And because of that, I'll be patient until you admit to me, and yourself, that you love me, too. The trust will follow."

This man was too good for her, the dimwit who had been ready to settle for a man she hadn't truly loved, Maggie conceded...to herself. But, whether or not she deserved him, his love, she wasn't about to be so foolish as to let him get away from her. She was going to grab him and hang on tight—for the rest of her life.

Putting action to thought, Maggie coiled her arms around his neck and clung.

"I already love you, Mitch," she said, her body springing to vibrant life at the touch, the feel of him pressing urgently against her. "That's why I was so damned scared."

"I knew that," he murmured, with supreme self-confidence. "That's why I only panicked a little bit when you said we had to talk."

Laughing together between rapidly heating kisses, Maggie and Mitch made their slow, sense-arousing way up the stairs to his apartment, to his bed.

Two weeks before Christmas, Karla, now Mrs. Ben Daniels, gave birth to a healthy, squalling son.

Staring through the nursery window at the red-faced baby, Mitch circled an arm around Maggie's waist and drew her close to his side to whisper in her ear.

"I want one of those," he murmured, indicating the baby. "Marry me, Maggie."

Tears glistening in her eyes, Maggie turned her head to smile at him. "I thought you'd never ask."

The sound of Mitch's joyous laughter rang through the hospital corridors.

* * * * *

July 2000
BACHELOR DOCTOR
#1303 by Barbara Boswell

August 2000
THE RETURN OF ADAMS CADE
#1309 by BJ James
Men of Belle Terre

September 2000
SLOW WALTZ ACROSS TEXAS
#1315 by Peggy Moreland
Texas Grooms

October 2000
THE DAKOTA MAN
#1321 by Joan Hohl

November 2000
HER PERFECT MAN
#1328 by Mary Lynn Baxter

December 2000
IRRESISTIBLE YOU
#1333 by Barbara Boswell

MAN OF THE MONTH

For twenty years Silhouette has been giving
you the ultimate in romantic reads. Come join
some of your favorite authors in helping us to
celebrate our anniversary with the most rugged,
sexy and lovable heroes ever!

Available at your favorite retail outlet.

Where love comes alive™

Visit Silhouette at www.eHarlequin.com   SDMOM00-3

Silhouette —

where love comes alive—online...

eHARLEQUIN.com

your romantic
books

♥ **Shop online! Visit Shop eHarlequin and discover a wide selection of new releases and classic favorites at great discounted prices.**

♥ **Read our daily and weekly Internet exclusive serials, and participate in our interactive novel in the reading room.**

♥ **Ever dreamed of being a writer? Enter your chapter for a chance to become a featured author in our Writing Round Robin novel.**

• • • • • • •

your romantic
life

♥ **Check out our feature articles on dating, flirting and other important romance topics and get your daily love dose with tips on how to keep the romance alive every day.**

• • • • • •

your
community

♥ **Have a Heart-to-Heart with other members about the latest books and meet your favorite authors.**

♥ **Discuss your romantic dilemma in the Tales from the Heart message board.**

your romantic
escapes

♥ **Learn what the stars have in store for you with our daily Passionscopes and weekly Erotiscopes.**

♥ **Get the latest scoop on your favorite royals in Royal Romance.**

You're not going to believe this offer!

In October and November 2000, buy any two Harlequin or Silhouette books and save $10.00 off future purchases, or buy any three and save $20.00 off future purchases!

Just fill out this form and attach 2 proofs of purchase (cash register receipts) from October and November 2000 books and Harlequin will send you a coupon booklet worth a total savings of $10.00 off future purchases of Harlequin and Silhouette books in 2001. Send us 3 proofs of purchase and we will send you a coupon booklet worth a total savings of $20.00 off future purchases.

Saving money has never been this easy.

I accept your offer! Please send me a coupon booklet:

Name: _____

Address: _____ City: _____

State/Prov.: _____ Zip/Postal Code: _____

Optional Survey!

In a typical month, how many Harlequin or Silhouette books would you buy <u>new</u> at retail stores?

☐ Less than 1   ☐ 1   ☐ 2   ☐ 3 to 4   ☐ 5+

Which of the following statements best describes how you <u>buy</u> Harlequin or Silhouette books? Choose one answer only that <u>best</u> describes you.

☐ I am a regular buyer and reader
☐ I am a regular reader but buy only occasionally
☐ I only buy and read for specific times of the year, e.g. vacations
☐ I subscribe through Reader Service but also buy at retail stores
☐ I mainly borrow and buy only occasionally
☐ I am an occasional buyer and reader

Which of the following statements best describes how you <u>choose</u> the Harlequin and Silhouette series books you buy <u>new</u> at retail stores? By "series," we mean books within a particular line, such as *Harlequin PRESENTS* or *Silhouette SPECIAL EDITION*. Choose one answer only that <u>best</u> describes you.

☐ I only buy books from my favorite series
☐ I generally buy books from my favorite series but also buy books from other series on occasion
☐ I buy some books from my favorite series but also buy from many other series regularly
☐ I buy all types of books depending on my mood and what I find interesting and have no favorite series

Please send this form, along with your cash register receipts as proofs of purchase, to:
In the U.S.: Harlequin Books, P.O. Box 9057, Buffalo, NY 14269
In Canada: Harlequin Books, P.O. Box 622, Fort Erie, Ontario L2A 5X3
(Allow 4-6 weeks for delivery) Offer expires December 31, 2000.   PHQ4002

COMING NEXT MONTH

#1327 MARRIAGE PREY—Annette Broadrick
Until she found herself stranded on an isolated island with
irresistibly handsome police detective Steve Antonelli, red-hot
passion had just been one of overprotected Robin McAlister's
fantasies. Could her sizzling romance with an experienced man like
Steve develop into a lasting love?

#1328 HER PERFECT MAN—Mary Lynn Baxter
Man of the Month
Strong-willed minister Bryce Burnette and flamboyant
Katherine Mays couldn't have been more different. Only the fierce
desire and tender love this red-haired beauty was stirring up inside
Bryce would be able to dissolve the barriers that separated them.

#1329 A COWBOY'S GIFT—Anne McAllister
Code of the West
Rodeo cowboy Gus Holt had to do a whole lot more than turn on his
legendary charm if he wanted to win back the heart of schoolteacher
Mary McLean. He'd have to prove—in a very special way—that this
time he was offering her a lifetime of love.

#1330 HUSBAND—OR ENEMY?—Caroline Cross
Fortune's Children: The Grooms
Angelica Dodd was powerfully drawn to—and pregnant by—
charismatic bad boy Riley Fortune. But trusting him was another
matter. Could Riley open his hardened heart and show her that they
shared more than a marriage of convenience?

#1331 THE VIRGIN AND THE VENGEFUL GROOM—
Dixie Browning
The Passionate Powers/Body & Soul
Even his tough training as a navy SEAL hadn't given Curt Powers the
wherewithal to resist a virginal beauty like Lily O'Malley. He longed
to take Lily—to make her his woman. But much to this confirmed
bachelor's surprise, he also wanted to make her his *wife*.

#1332 NIGHT WIND'S WOMAN—Sheri WhiteFeather
The moment pregnant Kelly Baxter showed up at his door,
Shane Night Wind knew his life was forever changed. How could he
walk away from this woman in need? How could he protect his heart
when Kelly and her baby could be his only salvation?

CMN1000